Crush

DEADLY HEARTS, BOOK 1

EVE NEWTON

Crush

Deadly Hearts, Book 1

A Dark Contemporary Romance Novel

By Eve Newton

Copyright © Eve Newton, 2021

Preface

Author's Note:

Dear Reader,

Please note that this book contains heavy triggers of self harm, rape and mental distress. For reference the scene of rape is in Chapter 20 and it is a flash back in italics. This is not a graphic scene, it is more introspective, although you are aware of what is going on, the details are sparse. For reference, the most vivid act of self harm appears in Chapter 45 at the end of the chapter.

Please note, though, that this book is dark and includes scenes of BDSM, with power play, blood play and knife play.

Love Eve x

Chapter One

Ruby

I t's 7AM on a drizzly Wednesday morning when I walk into my Black Widow bar and nightclub. The six-inch heels of my patent black Christian Louboutins clack on the hardwood floor as I make my way, briefcase in hand, Coach purse slung over my shoulder across the walkway to my office. Sylvie is mopping the gross 'stick' off the floor from spilt beers and God only knows what else, the acrid smell of cleaner hitting my nose as I progress further into the depths of the darkened building. The black wall makes it even dimmer, an ambience that I prefer to brighter colors.

My two Doormen, Ramsey and Benn are sitting at the bar, having a drink after wrapping up work for the night. They are having yet another discussion of who the best English football team in Manchester is.

"Hey, Boss!" Ramsey calls over, spotting me instantly. He gives me a thorough, undisguised once-over, even though he knows I'm off limits. My tight black dress skims my curves nicely, the black overcoat needed for the Manchester rain is

1

hanging open and is expensive and well cut. I only ever wear two colors. Black for every day and red for nighttime.

Ramsey's eyes meet mine, filled with a raw lust which he quickly squashes. He is gorgeous. Six-five and built like a brick shithouse. Short dark hair and eyes to match, not many are fool enough, even piss drunk to take him on. "You're the decider, Boss. United or City?" he says, his tone dark and low.

Flicking my long black hair over my shoulder, I grin at him, ignoring the undertone. "There's no choice. United all the way."

Benn groans, closing his bright blue eyes and shaking his blond head. "Oh, lass," he says, his Scottish accent sending a tingle down my spine. "You are so wrong."

I laugh and protest. "I've got nothing against City. Pep's got himself a cracking team, but my heart belongs to United," I say and wave them off. "Now get gone. It's way past closing."

They both stand up, Benn only a tiny bit shorter than Ramsey but just as wide and they head off. I turn and stalk to my office, meeting my assistant, David on the way.

He gives me a bright smile and also gives me a once-over, but this is purely for fashion's sake. He is as gay as I am straight, and I adore him. "You are fabulous, Ruby Bellingham," he says and then hands me a mug of steaming black coffee. "Widow's brew, just for you," he sings.

"You're a prince among men," I practically pant and snatch it off him. It's hot and dark and my first sip slides down my throat like honey.

"Consider it a birthday gift. Commute a bitch?" he commiserates.

"You know it," I growl, wishing I didn't live so far out of the city. The traffic is a fucking nightmare. I narrow my eyes. "How did you know?"

He nods in agreement and then shrugs it off. "I know everything," he replies. "Don't forget your parents are ringing in about half an hour," he reminds me. "Don't be late. The time difference is an arsehole."

"It's only five hours to New York," I remind him. "And it's calling, not ringing."

"You live in England, you say ringing," he chides me, which is a regular occurrence. I grew up in New York and only moved here five years ago when I was twenty-one. I owe my parents everything. All four of them. Yeah, my mom has three husbands. I know Rex is my bio dad, but I love Lachlan and Alex as if they were my blood. My mom runs her own empire back in the States and lent me the money to get started out here. I paid them back within a year and now own five successful *legit* nightclubs and three not so lawful casinos. That's where my real money and power come from.

"BT-dubs...you need to head downstairs," David says.

I frown at him and stop in the middle of the corridor outside my office. "Why?"

"A game ran on. Beth can't get them out. She needs help."

"Fuck sake," I growl. "They know better than this and where the fuck is Tony?" I shove my briefcase and handbag at him and rip off my coat, throwing that onto the pile loaded in his arms.

"He clocked out at five," David says in disgust at the asshole who abandoned his post.

"Are you joking?" I snarl, beyond pissed off. "He just left Beth down there? Why didn't you call me sooner?"

David nods glumly. "I did!" he protests. "About fifty times."

"What?" I mutter and reach over to pull my phone out of my pocket. Dead. "Fuck! David! I forgot to charge it. Shit."

"Didn't want to recruit the legit squad unless it was absolutely necessary. They're just parked, nothing too raucous."

"Yeah, I hear you," I murmur. Ramsey and Benn don't

3

know about the underground casino, and I'd like to keep it that way.

"I'll sort this," I growl.

"Go get 'em, tiger," he drawls in a fake American accent.

I grimace at him, but he pays me no mind and saunters off to dump my stuff in my office. I turn and head further down the corridor, right to the end where it seemingly stops. As a necessary precaution, I glance over my shoulder, but there is no one there. I find the button which operates the sliding door, hidden in a knot in the wood paneling and press it. I stalk through and close the door, marching down the stairs as quickly as my heels will allow me to.

"Boys," I purr, sugarcoating my anger. "You know the rules...out by five."

"Ruby-roo!" a large, ugly man shouts at me. "Stakes are too high, babe. No one leaves until I've won all my money back."

I scowl at him. "Jake," I snap, walking over quickly to the poker table, where four other players are slumped over, desperate to get out of here. No one has made a move though, because Jake is one of Manchester's biggest gangsters and will kill anyone who even looks at him wrong. He doesn't scare me though. Not even close. "Pack it up now. Rules are rules for a reason, fuckface."

"Ouch," he chortles, his big fat face jiggling. "How about you come over here and fuck my face with that sweet pussy of yours."

"You wish," I snort, suppressing my shudder of disgust. I'd rather fuck a frog. Standing in between him and the quiet fellow parked next to him, his pudgy eyes land on my chest and I resist the urge to cross my arms over my fairly ample breasts. "Now pack it up."

"No one leaves until I've won my money back," Jake says in a tone that he is probably used to people obeying. Not me,

4

though. Fuck that. I'm about to start sweeping the table clear, when his fat hand slips under my dress and lands on my thigh. He gets as far as trailing it upwards a few millimeters before I stop him. I hike up the other side of my dress and pull out the switch blade I always carry strapped in a thigh-holster. I bring my hand with the blade up to his neck and flick the switch. The steel snaps out against his throat and the room goes quiet.

"Remove your hand before I do it for you," I say quietly, calmly.

"Whoa," he says, taking his hand back and holding it up with the other one. "Calm your tits, sweetheart. It's just a bit of fun."

"Pack your shit up and get out of my casino," I say in the same steady tone as before.

He now knows I mean business and relents, finally. "No need to get all hormonal," he grouses, which enrages me to the point where if Beth hadn't been hovering on the other side of the table, I'd have stabbed him in the heart for being a chauvinistic pig. With a white-knuckled grip on the handle of the knife, I lower it slowly and flick the blade back in. I cast my steely green-eyed gaze at the four other members of this underground poker game and say, "If any of you stay past five again, you are banned, got it?"

"Yes, ma'am," they all mutter under their breaths, relieved to be set free from Jake's menace.

"You're such a bitch," Jake mutters, hauling his enormous frame out of the creaking chair.

"If you find my company so unpleasant, don't bother coming back," I retort, slipping the knife back into the holster. "Get outside and dissipate like fucking ghosts."

I fold my arms and watch them head towards the back door which leads out into the dingy alley at the back of the nightclub.

"It's clear," David says, coming down the stairs, studying

5

his iPad which has the security camera feed on it. "Go on now." He shoos them away like annoying geese and gives me a big smile. "Have I told you lately how fabulous you are?" he says.

"Can never hear it enough," I say, finally relaxing as the last of the lingerers fucks off and slams the door behind them.

Beth lets out an unsteady breath and tries to brush past me. I grab her upper arm. "Did he hurt you?" I ask. She is shaken, badly. Her pretty face is pale and her usually tight blonde ponytail is loosened slightly.

She shakes her head. "Nah, he's a twat, but he doesn't touch."

I find that *very* hard to believe. If he copped a feel of *my* leg, I'm pretty sure he tried something worse with my croupier. But until she admits it, there is nothing I can do. I soften my expression as much as I can. "You know you can tell me," I murmur.

She yanks her arm out of my grip. "Nothing to tell," she says shortly, and turns her back. The shine of tears I caught a glance of tells me everything I need to know.

That fucker. I clench my hand into a fist. I'm just looking for an excuse to take him down. He has been sniffing around my business for years.

"Parents," David says, interrupting my murderous thoughts.

"Get me that short list as soon as possible. Tony is done here," I order David.

He nods and turns and heads back up the stairs. With a last look back at Beth, I grit my teeth and follow him. She won't speak up because she is afraid, but it's Jake who should be afraid. They don't call me the Black Widow for nothing. I have absolutely *no problem* getting my hands dirty.

I stalk back up the stairs and plaster a smile on my face. Disappearing into my office, I sit at my desk and lift the lid of my laptop. Straight away it beeps for an incoming video call, and I answer it with a bright, "Hey, Mom."

My mom and three dads are all squished into the couch at home, waving frantically at me, as they sing Happy Birthday, making me laugh. I wish I could tell them who I really am, but they will never understand my need for power and the thrill that my dangerous life gives me. The edge of not knowing what lies around each corner makes my clit twitch.

It's my secret to keep, so they are safe from the darkness that lurks around every corner in my world. If only they knew the biggest darkness was me.

Chapter Two

Ruby

Searching through the short list again a few hours later, I figure I've got the best three out of the ten best Doorman in the city. They are all discreet, have good references and have worked the underworld business for a while. I have certain allies and we share information, but the likes of the East side gang are not my friends. I would even go so far as to say they are my enemies. They want to bring me down, but I'm untouchable right now. That may not last which is what makes this so exciting. Keeping one step ahead, always looking over my shoulder and sleeping with one eye open.

I live for it.

"Yeah, these three," I say eventually to David, who is waiting patiently for my decision. "Contact them and tell them it's an immediate interview with a view to immediate start. If they're not interested, they can fuck off and will be removed from the short list. Got it?"

"On it," David says and disappears to make the phone calls.

Sitting back, I relax as much as I can. Jake has really wound me up tight and I could do with a release of tension. I'm surprised when there is a soft knock on the door. David usually just barges in unless he knows I'm in a meeting.

"Yeah?" I call out, sitting forward again, my shoulders tensing back up.

The door opens a crack and Ramsey sticks his head around it. "You busy?" he asks.

I shake my head. "Not right now. Shouldn't you be home sleeping though?"

"I had an hour. Will grab another one later. Not much for sleeping," he says and enters fully, shutting the door behind him with his foot.

Interesting. "Same," I say lightly. "You'd get on with my dad. He's the worst insomniac there is."

He smiles and then walks slowly forward.

"So what's up?"

He pauses mid-way to my desk and produces his hand from around his back. Balanced on his fingertips is a square box, wrapped up in birthday paper. "Happy Birthday," he says, presenting it to me by placing it lightly on the desk.

"How did you know?" I grimace at him, but it all becomes clear seeing as I asked that very question not that long ago to my meddlesome assistant.

"David," he confirms with a laugh, which lights up his dark eyes. "Don't be mad at him. I pestered the shit out of him."

"I see," I murmur and reach out to pull the box closer to me. Don't get me wrong, I like my birthday, I just don't want the whole of the underworld to suddenly find out I'm only twenty-five, now twenty-six years old. I try to present an older air, so they don't think I'm some airhead who just fell out of college.

I lift the lid suspiciously, half expecting something to jump out at me, but instead when I look down into the deep box, I see a small black Pangolin Fixed Blade knife. With a raised eyebrow, I pick it up and examine it.

"Nice," I murmur, meeting his eyes. "Why this?" I mean, I know why I want it, but how does he know I want it?

He gives me a steady gaze and says, "Because if you are dealing with the likes of Jake Noonen, then I want you safe."

I lick my lips slowly and place the knife down on the table. "How do you know I deal with Jake Noonen?" I ask carefully. We are treading in very dodgy waters here.

"I know all about the downstairs to this club, Ruby," he says, my name sounding sweet coming from his lips. He usually calls me 'Boss'. "I know who comes and who goes. I've made it my business to know."

"Why? So you can hold it over me?" I ask, a hint of danger dropping into my tone.

"So I can keep you safe," he says.

"I see," I murmur, wondering if he is on the up and up. "You know that you aren't supposed to know. Does Benn know?"

Ramsey shakes his head. "Nope, just me. Now do you want the second part to your present?"

"There's a part two?" I ask surprised.

He nods and pulls something out of his back jeans pocket and bunches it in his fist. I take a moment to check him out. He is wearing a black t-shirt which shows off his rock-hard body and a black duster coat that he rocks like a god. The atmosphere has gone slightly tense as he approaches me slowly, coming around to my side of the desk.

I swivel in my chair so that I'm facing him when he stops inches away from me.

He holds his hand out in front of me. "Stand up," he says quietly.

I hesitate. I'm not used to men telling me what to do, especially in my own office. I purse my lips, but then decide to go with it and place my hand in his large one. It closes over mine and he helps me out of my chair.

I let out a small gasp when he drops to his knees in front of me. I start to panic. What is this? What is he doing? My palms sweat and I'm about to give him a swift kick so that I can back up when he reaches out to place his hand on either side of my dress at the hem.

My breathing goes heavier at his touch. I stand stock still as I wait to see what he is going to do, knowing I can get out of this if things go sour. He slowly slides his hands up, bunching my dress up as he trails up my outer thighs until my dress is up around my hips. My clean-shaven pussy is visible to him through the scant lace of my thong, but I don't care right now. He is turning me on with whatever he is doing.

To my surprise, he doesn't even give my pussy a glance. He meets my eyes and holds up the item that was in his hand.

I start to pant slightly. I open my legs a little bit so that he can reach around to strap the new thigh-holster to my right thigh. His fingers brush lightly over my skin and I'm disappointed when he finishes up and removes his hands. He leans over to scoop up the knife. He traces the blade of the knife over the sensitive skin of my inner thigh, drawing it upwards until he reaches the holster. I hold my breath, waiting for the burn of being cut, but it doesn't come. He is gentle, even though the action is dark, and I want it more than anything in that moment. I can taste it. He slides it slowly into the holster, his eyes burning with desire. It's only when he reaches for the hem of my dress that his fingers skate over my lace-covered pussy for a second before he pulls the dress back down. It's the only indication I have that he even saw what was in front of him.

He stands up and I press my legs together. I've gone damp from his slight touch, which startles me. Not many men have been able to work me with a small act, even one that was sexy as fuck and has left me wanting more even though he is my employee, and I can't go there with him.

"Thanks," I murmur, looking up at him from my foot shorter stature. He is immense. I suddenly feel the need to be held by him.

"Anytime," he murmurs back, his intense gaze boring into mine. "Now I know you're doubly safe."

"You shouldn't care much about that," I whisper.

"Oh, but I do," he says and backs off. "See you tonight."

"Yeah," I rasp, watching him leave my office with me in a state of arousal that must be dealt with immediately.

"Oh! By the way," he says, poking his head back around the door.

I hope he's here to finish the job, but no such luck. It's all business now.

"I heard about Tony leaving," he says, making me frown.

How does he know about Tony *and* that he left?

"I know a guy. He is sound. Discreet and gets the job done. I can send him over later."

"Oh?" I ask, my arousal taking a nosedive. "You don't want it yourself?" The bite in my tone is obvious, but he ignores it.

"I like my job at front of house. Layton is used to back room work. I'll send him over."

"Sure," I murmur, seemingly having no choice as Ramsey has now left and I have no intention of running after him, even if it is to berate him for being an overbearing asshole that has stuck his nose into my business where it definitely does not belong. This Layton guy can show up, but I don't have to see him. Simple as that.

I sit down, feeling the dampness still between my legs. I cross them and clear my throat, pushing Ramsey and his sudden knowledge of my underworld work away to deal with later. And make no mistake, it *needs* dealing with.

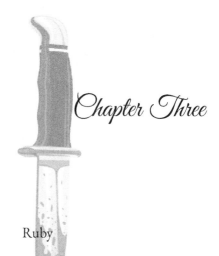

Chapter Three

Ruby

I glare at David standing in the doorway of my office with a big grin on his face. *Layton* is standing behind him looking bored as fuck. He is something else to look at though. He is roughly the same size as Ramsey but with pitch black hair and blue eyes that are practically luminous. Contacts? Nah. He doesn't appear to be the vain type. I can see most of him around David's slim frame and he is dressed in jeans and a long sleeve t-shirt with some kind of emblem blazoned onto the front, along with a black leather jacket. If he told me now he drives a motorbike, I wouldn't be surprised.

"You were expecting him, apparently," David explains unnecessarily.

"Not exactly," I growl, but gesture for him to come in anyway. I've already interviewed two of *my* guys and had already decided on one unless the third one was out of this world spectacular. This is just a waste of my time.

Layton saunters in, arrogant without a care in the world and plonks himself down opposite me. David backs out, laughing silently at me with some untold joke that he and his new buddy, Ramsey have probably got going. He shuts the door and I turn to Layton with a grimace.

He thrusts a piece of paper at me, and I give it a cursory glance before I do a double take and look closer.

"You used to work for Scott?" I ask, wondering why he isn't on the shared information sheet.

"Yep."

I wait for more, but nothing comes. "Why did you leave?" I ask tightly.

"I smashed a guy's face in, and he didn't approve." Blue eyes find mine with a challenging stare which I don't back down from.

"Care to share why you did that?" I question.

"He was a little prick who thought he could cop a feel of some woman's tits without her permission. I disagreed."

Oh, did you now? Okay, so I'll admit that my heart starts to beat a little bit faster. There is nothing sexier than a man who will stand up for a woman when they are being assaulted by little pricks. Or big ones, I think furiously about Jake the snake.

"Is that a deal breaker? You look like the type of woman who would break my nuts over it." His smile is sinister and my heart thumps louder.

"You clearly have no idea who I am," I say darkly.

"Oh, I know who you are," he says, leaning forward. "Black Widow. Your rep is legendary. I'm just messing with you."

I narrow my eyes. "About the reason you stopped working for Scott or about me breaking your nuts?"

"Breaking my nuts. I know you'll approve. I heard..." He stops and gives me a curious look. "You're smaller than I thought."

"Excuse me?" I choke out.

"You took down Eddie Santo with your bare hands. I don't see it with you sitting there in that fancy dress."

"Eddie," I growl. "He also had a problem with hands going where they shouldn't."

"And so you crushed them. I approve."

"Gee, thanks," I drawl. "Because I was soooo seeking your validation."

He snorts. "Ramsey wasn't lying when he said you had bite. I like you. I'll come and work here."

"Oh, will you?" I exclaim. "I didn't offer you the job."

"Look, love. There is no one better for this job than me. We are aligned with how we like to deal with...situations, so I know you won't tell me how to do my job."

"Hmm," I murmur and pick up my now charged phone. I quickly fire off a text message to Scott asking for a reference, outside of the incident with which they parted ways.

We stare at each other while I wait for Scott to reply. The little dots are flashing so I know he's replying but it seems to be taking a while.

"How do you know Ramsey?" I ask eventually.

"We went to school together. Used to smoke behind the bike sheds."

I stifle my laugh because I used to do the same. "Oh, so you know each other well?"

He nods, his eyes wandering around my office. "You from New York?" he asks.

"Yep. Born 'n bred."

"Nice," he says. "Always wanted to visit the Big Apple."

My phone suddenly beeps into the few seconds of silence, and I grab it like a lifeline. For some reason I cannot figure out, this man knocks me off my game. In fact, around him I have *no* game.

"Well?" he asks as I read Scott's lengthy message about

how Layton is a good bloke, but a bit bloodthirsty even for this type of work.

"You carry a weapon?" I ask, still staring at my phone.

"No need," he says, thumping his ginormous fists lightly on my desk.

"Think very highly of your fighting skills, don't you?"

"Did you not read all the way down to the bottom?" he replies, slightly confused, indicating the paper in front of me which passes for a dark version of a resumé.

Embarrassed to be caught out that in fact, no I didn't read anything past his last source of employment, I snatch it up and scan all the way down, my mouth going dry.

"Sniper for the SAS," I say, nodding my head. "Aren't you supposed to be all hush-hush about that?"

"In the normal world. This isn't normal. Read on."

"MMA World Champion three years running," I say, mildly impressed. Okay, hella impressed, but c'mon. This dude does not need more ego stroking. "Black belt in three different martial arts and taught Krav Maga by the head of Israeli Special Forces."

"Still think I need a weapon?"

"Probably not, but the people I do business with are..."

"Nothing I can't handle," he says. "So do I start or what?"

"Can you be back here by seven?"

He nods once and rises. "If you ever fancy showing me exactly *how* you took down Eddie, I'd be up for it," he says, that bold blue gaze practically making me cream my lacy thong.

"Maybe," I murmur and watch him go, wishing with everything I have that I'd told him he didn't get the job so that I could slam him up against the wall of my office and climb him like a tree.

Sadly, I do not get involved with my employees.

It only leads to trouble.

17

With that important issue dealt with, I call David into my office as I stand up.

"Going somewhere?" he asks.

"Yeah, I need to go...do something," I say, deciding not to tell him that I need to take care of the lady boner that has sprung up since Ramsey's little gift and Layton's badass attitude. It's been a week since I had time to visit the BDSM club that I'm a member of and that is six days too long. I need the thrill and the relief that comes from a visit, and I know myself well enough to know that if I don't go now, I will snap and probably murder the next asshole who walks through my door.

"That's vague," David mutters. "Will you be coming back?"

"Uh-huh," I say. "Shouldn't be longer than a couple of hours." I turn my back as I gather up my coat and handbag. "See you in a bit."

He nods and waves me off.

I walk unsteadily down the corridor and out into the club. My hands are shaking, my shoulders aching from the tension that has sprung up. I grip the handle of my bag and head out into the fresh air. I breathe in deeply, my face turned towards the gray sky that is still crying tears of cold rain, but I'll walk to where I'm going. It's only ten minutes and by the time I get there, my head will be straight, and I can enjoy the time out as a Sub instead of storming in there as a Mistress. It's not what my body wants. It's not what my head needs. I need to be punished and the only one who can do that awaits just a ten-minute walk away.

Chapter Four

Ruby

Entering the club a few minutes later, I shed my coat and hand it in at the coat check along with my handbag. I feel myself relax instantly now that I'm here. My needs are about to be met and that's all I can focus on right now.

"Ruby," Giselle, the club owner says, coming over to me.

"Hey," I say, "How's things?"

"Good," she says. "How's your dad?"

I smile. "He's fine. Still wants to buy you out," I joke. Lachlan has owned New York's hottest sex club for years. I think my parents are into the lifestyle, but I've never seen it and neither has my sister, Scarlet. It's definitely not something I will ever bring up so unless they mention it, I will happily remain clueless as to the answer to this.

"Ha," she says. "He wishes. So, what can I do for you today?" she adds, getting down to business.

"DD/LG," I murmur, curling my hair behind my ear. I

need that extra care after I've been punished. I'm craving it. It's eating at me. "Is he here?"

She nods, a slight smile on her face. "He has been waiting for you."

I breathe out in relief and follow her as she heads deeper into the dark club. I ignore all the other activities going on around me. I'm hyper focused on where I need to be, to the point where I want to shove Giselle out of the way to get there quicker. Not only is it super rude, but part of the running of this club is that she hand delivers all her clients and picks them up when they're done.

When we reach door number six, I inhale as she knocks once and opens it. She steps back to let me pass and I enter the room filled with a deep red glow. I kick my shoes off straight away, feeling the plush black carpet under my feet. Giselle closes the door, leaving me alone with *him*. I have no idea who he is in real life, and I don't want to. All I know is that I need him in *this* part of my life. He gives me exactly what I want. He is standing with his back facing me, staring down at the equipment laid out on the sideboard that runs along the back of the room. There is a huge bed in the corner and chains attached to the walls. I look up at the large hook that dangles from the ceiling, and I exhale slowly. I reach around and unzip my dress, slipping it off my shoulder to drop on the floor. I slowly remove my bra and thong and then I turn to him, head lowered.

"Daddy," I purr quietly.

"Princess. Where have you been? I've been waiting for you." His soft Irish accent sends a tingle over my skin. I want to hear more of his voice. I want him to talk harshly to me before he croons lovingly.

"I'm sorry," I murmur. "I was held up."

He turns around, his face covered with a Phantom of the Opera type mask. I breathe steadily as he walks over to me, his bare feet in sharp contrast to his black suit pants and crisp white shirt.

"Explain," he says sternly when he reaches me. He leans over and attaches a black leather collar to my neck with a long leash, which he grips tightly.

"I lost track of time while I was playing on the swing," I whisper.

"I missed you," he says, his fingers twirling around my loose hair.

"I missed you too."

He drops the leash and scoops my hair up on top of my head and ties it up into a neat bun.

Then he picks up the leash again and mutters, "On your knees, Princess."

I drop to my knees, and he tugs on the leash, forcing me onto all fours to crawl after him when he walks to the middle of the room.

"You know better than to keep me waiting, Princess."

"I'm sorry," I whimper.

"Stand up."

I rise.

He attaches the leash to the big hook dropping from the ceiling. He walks away back to the sideboard and picks something up. Coming back to me, he attaches the nipple clamp to my aching peaks and then leaves me again.

"Have you been a good girl or a bad girl while you've been gone?" he asks.

"Bad," I whisper, eyes lower. "So bad."

"Tell me why you say that," he demands.

I cannot lie. There's no reason to. "I had murderous thoughts about a pig who touched my friend without her permission."

He spins back to me quickly, his head tilted. "Oh?"

"I'm sorry."

"Don't be, Princess. He sounds like he deserves your wrath."

I look up at him without meaning to. I wasn't expecting that. I was expecting, hoping for even, a harsh reprimand.

I quickly lower my eyes again and stay silent.

He approaches me again and holds out the riding crop he has in his hand. He rubs it gently against my pussy, pressing down on my clit. I moan as it feels so good, I need more. He pulls it away.

"Bad girls don't get to come," he says, but his tone is different. I can't quite figure it out.

"Please, Daddy," I beg him. "I need it."

"You want to be punished first?"

"Yes, I need to be punished for being so bad."

"No," he says suddenly and drops to his knees in front of me. I stumble back as this is odd. What is he doing?

His hands skim over the two knives still attached to my thighs before he runs his fingertip over the thin white ribbons of long-ago scars at the tops of my thighs. "You hurt yourself, Princess."

"I deserved it," I say carefully. This is treading into a territory I'm unfamiliar with.

"You have a darkness in you. So do I," he says quietly, then he leans forward and brushes his lips softly over the scars, his tongue flicking out and tasting my skin.

"Stop it," I cry out. "I'm bad! I'm a bad girl! I need to be punished!" I'm starting to panic. He has stopped the role play, and this has turned into something else entirely. It's twisted my mind and I don't know how to deal with this.

"No," he says again. "You just want to be loved. Let me love you."

"What?" I spit out and stumble back further. "What are you doing? This isn't what I came here for."

"Isn't it?" he asks, standing up again.

"No!" I yell.

He reaches up to unhook the leash and drops it. "If you don't want me to love you, you are free to leave," he says.

I stare at him in horror. He is fucking with me and it's cruel. Why is he doing this?

"You're kicking me out, Daddy?" I ask, scrambling to keep up the pretense even though it has crumbled all around me like a cookie castle.

"I want you to stay," he says steadily. "I know what you are seeking, Princess. Let me give it to you."

I shake my head. "This is all wrong," I moan, putting my hands to my head. "All wrong. Be my Daddy! I need my Daddy!" I lunge forward and beat my fists against his chest. He grabs my hands, pulling them away from him.

"Admit what you really want," he says, the dark tone chilling me to my core.

I stop struggling and yank my arms back. I spin and grab my dress and underwear and aim for the door.

He is there in a split second, his big hand holding it closed as I try to open it. "Tell me what you want. What are your darkest desires?"

"Why are you doing this?"

"Because you are stronger than you think you are. You are hiding from your feelings and that's why you come here."

"You don't know me!" I shriek at him. "You have absolutely no idea who I am or what I've done."

"I know more than you think, Ruby," he says, stopping me cold.

"How do you know my name?" I whisper, the dread and fear bubbling up inside me.

"I know you, Ruby," he says again. "Let me give you the love you deserve."

I don't move. I can't.

He lets go of the door and steps back. "If I'm wrong about what you want, then you are free to leave."

I hesitate and then I turn towards him. "Who are you?"

"Am I wrong?"

I shake my head slowly.

"Come, Princess. There will be no punishment today."

"Daddy," I cry, falling into his open arms.

We have landed back in familiar territory and the fact that he knows who I am, or at the very least he knows my name, doesn't matter anymore. Not while I'm in here. I'm safe.

He leads me to the bed and settles me in the middle, climbing onto it to hold me close for a few minutes before he lays me flat on my back and looms over me.

As quick as lightning, he pulls the two knives out of their holsters and lays them down.

I try to sit up, but he pushes me back. "You don't need them here, Princess. You are safe."

The rational side of me is screaming at me to run away from this *stalker* and never look back.

But the little girl inside me needs the comfort he is giving me.

The little girl wins.

Chapter Five

Ruby

He gathers me to him, close, wrapping his arms around me. I feel myself start to fall asleep, which is weird because I have never slept in someone else's arms before. It shows, though because as soon as he moves his hand to stroke my back, I come to, startled out of my daze.

"You're safe," he croons to me in that accent that I can't ignore. It's just too delicious for words.

"Please can we go back to why I came here?" I ask quietly.

He shakes his head. "No. I'm breaking roles," he says decisively and rolls me flat onto my back.

We've already done that. That feeling of panic rises up again at his words. What is he doing to me?

"Please, Daddy," I whisper.

"Stay still," he mutters and climbs off the bed. He returns a moment later with the riding crop he dropped when I tried to leave earlier.

Without a word, he lightly slaps the crop against my pussy, making me squirm. Okay, so this isn't exactly what I came here for, but it will do. I close my eyes and just feel. Every strike of the crop, every rub of my clit, every thrust of the handle when he shoves it inside me. I cry out, feeling the orgasm building deep within.

He pulls the crop away with a slight tut, leaving me on my edge, desperate for a release.

He lays the crop down and I feel like crying. But he turns me over onto my stomach. The nipple clamp that I'm still wearing bites into me, but I revel in the pain it brings. It is closer to the feeling I need from my visit here.

"Do not move at all," he instructs.

"Yes, Daddy," I murmur, a thrill going through me that he wants a living doll situation. I'm up for that. My body feels so heavy with exhaustion, confusion and pain right now anyway.

He parts my legs and once again slaps my pussy with the crop. This time a lot harder than the gentle touches from before. I bite my lip so I don't cry out. My cheek is plastered to the kitsch red satin covers as he tortured my pussy until I know it is red. He thrusts the handle into me again roughly and I scrunch my eyes tighter. He fucks my pussy hard and fast with the crop. My body tense, ready to come all over it, but he withdraws it, leaving me once again on the edge.

I want him to touch me, but he never does. I have never ridden his cock and right now I want it more than any cock I've ever had before.

"Please, Daddy," I moan. "I need you."

"Quiet!" he snaps at me and brings the crop down to strike across my back hard enough to make me buck.

I gasp as it hits the dark pleasure button deep inside me. I bunch my hands up into the sheet, but make no other sound or movement.

"Bad girls get punished," he says and strikes me again, but

this time less forcefully. I don't think he meant to lash me so hard the first time, not that I mind.

I feel the bed jostle under me and then a soft buzz as he turns on a vibrator. I smile into the sheet as he inserts it into my pussy, as far up as it will go and then lets it go. My eyes fly open as he brings down a softer whip onto my back than the rigid crop. I squirm, unable to help it. The vibrator is buzzing away merrily inside me all on its own and it's driving me to the point of an orgasm that I know is going to slay me in all the right ways.

He strikes me harder then. Each lash more forceful than the last.

"Bad girl," he mutters. "Bad, bad girl."

I whimper from the sheer pleasure overload and cry out, muffling it into the bed, as an orgasm crashes over me, sweeping me up in its depraved wave of ecstasy, making my body shudder uncontrollably as tears of relief seep out of my eyes.

"Thank you, Daddy," I weep, breathlessly. "Thank you."

He says nothing. He just climbs off the bed and then I hear the door open and close.

I freeze.

"Daddy?" I call out quietly. "Daddy?" It's louder this time, more frantic when he doesn't answer me.

I turn my head to see the room is empty.

He left me.

He abandoned me on this bed after punishing me. He isn't here to take care of me now, he left me all alone.

"No," I cry out. "Daddy, please come back. I'm sorry. I'm sorry I disappointed you. I'll try harder. Please! Please?"

But he doesn't return. The only sound in the room is my desperate sobbing, soaking the sheet under my face, and the vibrator still buzzing away inside my cunt.

I buck as another climax hits me. The emotional pain of

what he has inflicted on me, far worse than anything physical he has ever done, fuels the fire of the best orgasm I have experienced, as the blood courses through my veins. My body shakes violently, and I squirt all over the sheet. I'm sweating and panting, my pussy clutching and creaming the vibrator so fiercely, it borders on painful.

Then it's over.

And I'm all alone to clean up the mess I've made all over this bed.

Chapter Six

Ruby

There is a soft knock at the door, and I turn my head quickly, but the disappointment slams into me when Giselle pokes her head around.

"Ruby," she murmurs, coming in and closing the door.

I wipe my eyes on the sheet and sit up, pulling the vibrator out and throwing it in a rage against the wall.

"Ah!" I yell. "Where is he?"

"Hush," she says to me, climbing onto the bed with me. "He has gone."

Those three words cut me deep and my anger dissipates as quickly as it came to be replaced with sorrow again. "Why?" I ask quietly.

"Here," she says and reaches out to take the nipple clamp off. I gasp and then moan because *he* is supposed to take care of me now and he isn't here. He left me. Giselle rubs her palms over my aching peaks, soothing them gently.

I bat her hand away, not interested in her aftercare. "Where. Is. He?" I grit out.

"I don't know," she says. "But there are some things I must tell you."

"Oh? Like what a prick he is?" I spit out.

She shakes her head. "He knows who you are," she says in a rush. "He has known all along. He knew you came here, and he insisted that I set you up with him."

"What? That was months ago!" I blurt out.

She lowers her eyes. "I know. I'm sorry for the deception. He was...convincing."

"He threatened you?" I ask, confused. "Why? Why did he want me?"

"It doesn't matter, and I don't know, Ruby. I'm sorry. This is all my fault that you are hurting."

"Do you know why he left me here?"

Again, she shakes her head. "All I know is that he stormed out, saying he won't return."

"What? Never?" I ask in horror. Who will I come to when I need a release? "No," I say, shaking my head in denial. "No. He wouldn't do that."

Giselle is silent.

"You have no idea why he wanted me?"

"No, child. I wasn't in a position to ask, only to do as he said."

"How did he even know when I'd show up?" I ask, really expecting an answer, but she doesn't have one to give me. "Damn him. What is his name? Who is he?"

"All I know is that he is a powerful man, and he is not used to being denied. Tread carefully, Ruby. This warning is all I can give you now."

"Fuck you," I spit out, turning my rage and frustration onto the club owner. "How dare you deceive me like this! You were my *friend*." I grab the crop and leap off the bed, reaching for the discarded vibrator from the floor. I march over to the sideboard and yank open the bottom drawer. I pull out the cleaning wipes and set about wiping my cum from the instruments furiously.

"Ruby, please, do not be angry with me…"

"Shut your mouth," I growl, chucking the items into the drawer. These are mine. No one else will use them, not even me anymore. "I'm done with you and this place."

"Ruby, no," she says sadly.

"You have betrayed me, and you know what fucking happens to people who betray me?" I ask, stalking back over to the bed to snatch up my two knives. I make a slashing motion with my new Pangolin across my neck, and she pales. "Watch your fucking back, Giselle because you have just made a powerful enemy."

I turn from her, leaving the wet sheet seeing as she is still sitting on the bed, and scoop up my clothes again from the floor where they were dumped. I should've listened to my rational side. I should have run from here the second he said my name, but I was too caught up in my dark need to pay any attention to it. I was fooled.

No more.

I am nobody's fuck toy.

This asshole thinks he can treat me this way, he has another thing coming.

I stalk out of the room, stark naked, slipping my knives back into their holsters. When I reach the coat check I slip into my dress and shoes while I wait for my belongings and then shove my underwear into my handbag.

Marching defiantly out of the club and onto the street, I don't look back as Giselle runs after me. "Ruby! Wait, please!"

I will never return to her place of business, and I will make sure she is ruined before this month is done.

My temper is still hot a few minutes later as I round the corner of the street where Black Widow is. I'm startled when

I'm yanked roughly into the narrow alleyway that runs down the side of the club.

"What the fuck?" I growl, but have no time to assess the situation as I'm slammed face first into the alley wall, bruising my cheek and making my lip bleed. My attacker grips my left hand, crushing my bones, making me grunt.

"Jake sends his regards," the man breathes into my ear. I recoil from the stench of his breath and take a second to compose myself, shaking off the surprise and going into battle mode. He clearly knows about the stiletto blade attached to my left thigh, but there is no way he can know about my new gift from Ramsey. I slowly inch my dress up until I feel the holster and place my hand around the hilt of the blade.

"Yeah?" I snarl. "What does that fat fuck want this time?"

"He wants to see you dead, but first he wants to strip you bare," he growls, gripping the messy bun still on top of my head, ready to smash my face into the wall again.

"Ugh!" I spit out and bring my bent arm up to slam into my attacker's nose so that he stumbles backwards in shock.

"Fuck!" he cries. "You broke my fucking nose, you bitch!"

"That's not all I'm going to break," I tell him, gripping the handle of the knife tightly. He is too far away from me to lunge forward with any precision. I need to get in closer to send a message to Jake that you don't fuck with me.

The man, ugly and much taller than me, gets over his nose issue quickly as only a seasoned fighter can and dives forward, shoving me back up against the wall. I'm ready for it and hold my left hand out, keeping my blade hidden for now. He is surprised at my strength as I force him back with just one shove. I back it up with a knee to the groin, which doubles him over with a loud groan.

I reach out to grab his shiny shirt, my fist tight, the material biting into me. With all the force I can, I slam him up against the wall in this tight space.

"You tell Jake that if he wants me dead, he can come and do it himself and not send amateurs to do the job for him," I hiss at him and then I bring the knife up to his gut and stab him roughly in just the right place to miss his vital organs.

He grunts at the white-hot pain and slaps his hand to the wound as I twist the knife and lean harder on it.

"Got it?" I growl.

"Got it," he rasps.

I pull the knife out and let him go so that he slumps to the dirty, wet ground and I kick him for good measure.

He howls as my foot connects with the stab wound and then I spin on my heel, dropping the bloody blade into my handbag on top of my underwear. I drag the hair band out of my hair and my damp black hair tumbles around my shoulders. Snapping the hairband around my wrist, I walk steadily out of the alley the few short meters to the club door, my lip still bleeding and my cheek aching. I enter and go straight to my office, pushing David out of the way, who exclaims loudly and rushes after me.

"Ruby! Ruby! What happened? Are you okay?"

I ignore him and head into the en-suite bathroom attached to my office, glaring at my nasty appearance in the mirror with a groan of dented ego.

Chapter Seven

Ruby

"I'm fine," I grit out, beyond livid that I was jumped outside my own club. I mean what the fuck? It just adds insult to injury and pretty much sums up the shittiest day of the year so far.

"Do I need to call Michelle?" David asks hesitantly.

He knows calling the off the record doctor is a last resort.

"No, nothing broken. I'm fine," I say again, still glaring at my awful reflection.

"Ruby!" Ramsey's voice filters over David's head. "What the hell? What happened?"

"Nothing, I'm fine," I say absently.

"Fine usually means she is pissed off, but not quite ready to do anything about it yet," David stage-whispers to Ramsey.

I ignore him, but Ramsey shoves David out of the way and approaches me cautiously. "What happened?"

I huff out a breath and root around in my bag. I find the bloody knife and pull it out to dump in the basin. Somehow, my thong has tangled up with it and has also ended up in the basin. Ramsey glances at it briefly, his eyes going hard, his body going tense.

"It's not what it looks like," I say with an eye roll. "Stand down. But thanks for the birthday gift. Saved this from being a lot worse."

"Fuck, Ruby," he says, placing his large hand on my back.

I hiss and wince, pulling away as he agitates the whipping marks on my back.

"Tell me what happened," he says again, taking his hand away.

"I was coming back from a very shitty encounter and was attacked in the alleyway outside," I spit out. "One of Jake Noonen's boys. He is worse off," I add.

"Do we need to call the paramedics?" David asks carefully.

"No, he'll walk away. He's probably already gone, but he'll think twice about coming at me again. Asshole," I mutter.

"Jesus," Ramsey murmurs. "Ruby."

"Don't worry about it. Jake is a dickhead. I sent a message back to him to come after me himself if he wants me dead."

"I'll tell Layton not to let him in then," David says seriously.

I snort in amusement, hurting my battered cheek. "Ya think?"

"Fuck off," he mutters and disappears.

Unfortunately, he doesn't take Ramsey with him.

"Layton is already here?" I ask, grabbing a washcloth and running it under the cold tap. I press it to my bleeding lip.

"Yeah, he wanted the lay of the land," Ramsey says. "Ruby, I think you need private security. You are just asking for trouble."

"Don't get all overprotective," I snarl at him. "You have no right, and I can take care of myself."

"I know you can, but still, it wouldn't hurt," he insists. "I

35

care about you. I don't like seeing you like this." His eyes go back to the damp panties in the basin.

I snatch them up and drop them back in my bag. "I told you not to worry about that."

"Too late," he murmurs, meeting my gaze in the mirror. "Fuck it, Ruby. I've been playing by your rules since I started working here, but I'm done. Seeing you this way, knowing that I could've lost you...I want to be with you. There, I've said it." His grim face belies the passion in his tone.

Too bad I have to turn him down.

"I don't date employees. You know this. Everyone does." I drop the washcloth in the basin and scoop my hair up into a ponytail, snapping the hair band around my wrist into my hair briskly.

"I'm not talking about dating you," he says gruffly. "And if that's the case, then I quit."

I grimace at him and brush past him to walk back into my office. "Don't be an idiot," I snap. "I need you on the door. You're one of the best."

"One of?" he asks, a comically disappointed expression on his face.

"Need an ego stroke right now?" I ask. "Fine, you're the best. I refuse your attempt to quit, are we clear?" I fold my arms over my chest to glare at him.

He clenches his jaw, glaring back at me, those dark eyes simmering with frustration and disappointment that I've turned him down.

Well, tough.

I don't need him or anyone to distract me from my goal, my *need* to stay on top. The second I let my guard down, I'll be wiped out and I'll be damned if I let that happen. Relationships are a no-go for me. I don't want one. I don't need one. I'm happy with casual encounters and my arrangement at Giselle's.

I growl, concerning Ramsey further.

Former arrangement at Giselle's.

"David!" I yell.

He rushes in with Layton behind him, who has clearly been informed of my situation because he looks like he is about to murder someone.

"What is it?" David asks.

"Can you find out everything you can on Giselle Marchand. Both personally and her business. I mean a deep dive. I want to know what she fucking had for breakfast on July 1st, 1996, got it?"

He nods. "On it."

I let out a sigh of relief that he didn't question me over the whos and whys. He just did it. It's one of the reasons I love him.

"Let Layton drive you home, at least," Ramsey says quietly, seemingly brushing off my harsh rejection of him.

"Fine," I say, just to end this conversation and so that I have an excuse to get out of here. "Give me a minute."

I head back into the bathroom and close the door. I lean against it, eyes closed, taking a few deep breaths before I push off and walk over to the basin. I pick up the bloody knife and stick it under the hot tap. I turn it on and the water gushes out, rinsing the blood off for it to swirl down the drain along with all of my feelings over today's shitshow.

When I look up again into the mirror, I'm back.

I slip the blade back into the holster, snatch up my bag and head out. "Let's go," I say to Layton, ignoring Ramsey and David as I storm out of my office and into the parking lot at the back of the club, Layton trailing after me.

I wait, tapping my foot impatiently for him to catch up. It occurs to me belatedly that Nate will be expecting my call to Uber me home. I pull out my phone and send him a text as

Layton extends his arm and clicks the remote key to a sleek black Merc SL that makes me giggle.

"That's your car?" I ask, almost mocking him.

"What of it?" he growls, opening the passenger side door for me.

"Nothing for someone like me. You? I had you pegged as a biker."

He grunts. "Who says I'm not?" he asks. "Just get in."

I do as bid, and slip into the vehicle, waiting for him to join me.

"Where to?" he asks, gunning the engine.

I give him my address in Prestbury, one of the most exclusive places to live in the Greater Manchester area. I adore my house, but I'm on the verge of needing a place in the city so that my commute is less of a chore.

I sit back, glad that Layton is the strong silent type and enjoy the ride home.

Chapter Eight

Ruby

L ayton walks me to the front door of my sprawling ground level house, after I let us onto the property, and he parked up.

"You really don't have to..." I start, but he silences me with a fierce glare.

I smile to myself and check my watch. I bite the inside of my lip and open the front door. I step inside, my heels clacking on the Italian tile and dump my bag and coat on the floor and turn around. Kicking off my shoes, I face him with a sultry look that has him scowling at me.

I hike my dress up my thighs and say, "You know, you don't start working for me for another hour."

"And?" he growls.

I don't bother answering, I just grab his shirt and drag him inside, clapping my hand on the back of his neck to pull him down to my mouth. I sweep my tongue over his lips as they crash against mine and he opens up, plunging his tongue into my mouth with a noise that sounds like a lion's purr.

It sends a sensation of pure lust straight to my clit.

He takes a step back and regards me closely. "You know that Ramsey is in love with you, don't you?"

"So?" I ask, knowing how harsh that sounds, but can't let myself think about him right now.

"So I don't like hurting my friends."

"And?"

"And if I do this, it will hurt him."

"I'm your friend and I'll be hurt if you *don't* do this," I retort.

He shakes his head with a sigh. "You don't want to be with me, love. I like it rough."

If he was trying to put me off, he just did the complete opposite. With a soft moan, I grab his shirt again and press myself against his body, feeling his erection digging into me. "You don't scare me," I whisper in his ear.

"Fuck's sake," he mutters and then seemingly decides to get on with it. His big hand lands on the back of my neck to hold me close as he kisses me with a forcefulness that leaves me panting for more. His other hand reaches up for the zipper at the back of my dress and he slides it down slowly, enticingly. I moan into his mouth as he lets me go and slips it over my shoulders. He breaks the kiss, his gaze dropping to take in every inch of my naked body.

"Fuck, you're gorgeous," he murmurs, taking a step forward.

I quickly take a step back and then another until my back hits the wall behind me. The open plan room sprawls out in front of me, but it's blocked from my view as he looms into frame. He slowly turns me around and presses me up against the cool wall, my nipples peaking at the chill.

He hisses when he sees the marks left by my encounter at Giselle's, his fingers grazing over the light welts gently. He moves in closer, his body pushing me further into the wall.

"Are you sure you want this?" he asks quietly.

I nod, unable to speak.

"I need to hear you say it, Ruby," he says.

"Say what?" I rasp, my voice hoarse with need.

"Do you consent?"

"Fuck, yes," I breathe. "Yes, I consent."

He reaches around to cup my pussy before he squeezes and then takes my clit in his fingers to pinch and twist until I gasp with pure longing. Layton slips a finger inside me, thrusting roughly before I bat his hand away and turn around. He gathers me to him, kissing me again, lifting my leg up to wrap around his waist. I leap up, wrapping my other leg around him, his hands going to my ass to hold me to him. I snake my hand in between us and unzip his fly, sliding my hand into his jeans. His cock is enormous and rock-hard as I take it in my hand, stroking him with a purr of need. He walks backwards, his mouth never leaving mine until we reach the couch and then he drops me, reaching down to pull the Pangolin out of the holster strapped to my thigh. He trails the sharp edge up my stomach, not hard enough to draw blood, but hard enough to leave a red welt. The sting has me trembling in front of him, watching him closely as the knife makes its way up in between my breasts. He stops for a moment and then drags the blade under the swell of my right breast, circling it until he gets to the top. He repositions the knife so that the pointed tip is digging into my skin. He increases the pressure enough so that a tiny drop of blood forms through my broken skin.

I whimper with desire as I watch it slowly roll down over my nipple.

His clear blue eyes are transfixed to the droplet. After a moment, he drags the knife down to my nipple, flicking the aching peak, smearing the blood away before he leans down to take the bud in his mouth. He bites down roughly, making me

EVE NEWTON

squirm. I am soaking wet between my legs. I can feel the juice running down my thighs. I have never been turned on quite so seductively and in such a dark way before.

It is thrilling.

Layton drops the knife to my pussy, and I gasp in surprise when he lightly but quickly slaps the flat of the blade against me. I cry out, throwing my head back. I open my legs further, eager to have him in between them, but instead of his cock, he thrust the handle of the blade up my cunt, thrusting deeply until his hand is pressing against my wet heat.

"I want to feel you," he growls softly. "Do I need to cover up?"

"No," I pant. "I'm good."

He withdraws the handle of the knife and licks it clean before he slides it back into the holster. "Me too," he says and turns me around again, pushing me over the back of the couch. He settles in between my legs, his tip at my entrance.

I let out a long, loud moan as he eases his huge cock inside me right up to the hilt. He is enormous both in length and girth and my knees threaten to buckle under the pleasure he is giving me. I wiggle my ass and he smacks it. I yelp, but wiggle again so he will repeat the process. He does. His strong hand, giving me a proper resounding smack before he runs his hand tenderly over the hot spot. He doesn't move for a few seconds, just letting his cock fill me up, but then he grabs my hips and withdraws almost completely before he roughly slams back into me, shoving the couch forward with his vigor.

"Fuck, yes!" I cry out. "That's it. Fuck me hard."

He grunts, digging his fingers into my hips, bruising me, but I don't care. I want to feel the bite of pain before the pleasure takes over completely, sweeping me up in the tidal wave of ecstasy that crashes to shore moments later, only to swell up again, making my knees buckle. He lets go of my right hip and bunches his fist into my ponytail. He wraps it around his hand and pulls back, arching my back.

"Fuck, Ruby," he pants, pulling harder on my hair until I'm upright and crying out for more.

His other hand closes around my throat and he squeezes gently. Automatically, my hands go up to his and that's when he increases the pressure, choking me while he fucks the living daylights out of me.

"Fuck, yes, sweetheart," he mutters. "You are so fucking hot."

"Back at you," I cough out when he releases his hold on me and grabs my hips again. He shoves me away slightly, so his cock slips out and turns me around. He lifts me up and then straight down onto his cock to ride him in the middle of my sitting room, like a cowgirl on her last day on Earth.

Another climax thunders over me, clutching his cock, milking him until he can't hold on any longer. With a roar of triumph, he detonates inside me, filling me up with his cum until it slides back out and down my thighs.

Panting, I plant a kiss on his lips and climb off him, fully expecting him to pull up his pants and leave. Instead, he picks me up, cradling me in his massive arms, nuzzling my neck softly.

"I'll run you a warm bath," he says and heads in the direction of the corridor on the opposite side of the sitting room which clearly leads to the bedrooms.

I frown at him. "You don't have to do that," I say, wondering what the hell he is doing.

"Ruby," he says. "I may not have been responsible for the marks on your back, but I've hurt you and I know how to take care of my woman."

"Your woman now, am I?" I ask with a laugh as he makes his way down the long corridor to my bedroom, where I gestured despite my protest.

"Whether you have me as your man again or not, I'll always do the right thing," he says, almost affronted that I dare to think otherwise.

Suddenly, I feel a shift deep inside me. I may not know this man at all, but the parts I've seen of him are undeniably arousing. He has given me everything that I wanted tonight. Everything that I was craving and that has built up over an incredibly stressful day. I want to keep him around, but...

"Layton?"

"Yes, Ruby?"

"You're fired," I snort with a loud laugh as he drops me lightly on my bed and shakes his head at me, chuckling softly as he makes his way into the en-suite to run me a deep, warm bath.

Chapter Nine

Ramsey

I'm supposed to be on the door already. The bar is full. It won't turn into a club until 11PM, but there are still dickheads getting pissed up drunk, and disorder often ensues. They'll never learn. I'm not a big drinker, never was, never will be. One beer after work with Benn and that's it for me. But right now, I'm settling into panic mode, so the shot of whiskey in front of me is to calm my anxiety.

Layton should've been back ages ago.

He was supposed to drop Ruby off, see her into her home and then come back here. I'm bordering on terrified that they got ambushed and Ruby has been abducted or worse. Not many can get past Layton but it's not unheard of. No one is infallible.

"Is she back yet?" David asks, hurrying over to me and cozying in between me and the bloke next to me. He ignores the filthy look and gives me one of concern. "I can't reach Ruby or Layton on their mobiles."

"Me either," I reply, my blood running cold. This is

getting worse. I reach for the shot glass and down it in one gulp, feeling the burn as the peaty alcohol slides down my throat.

"Hey," Layton's voice sounds behind me.

I spin and grab him by the coat. "Is she okay?" I ask desperately.

"She's fine," Layton says. "Sleeping. David," he turns to the smaller man.

Sleeping?

"Yeah?" David says.

"Ruby fired me. She asked if you can get the other guy to come in...Andy, is it? If he can't start tonight, then Ramsey is to fill in."

"Fired?" David asks, scrunching up his nose. "Why? What did you do?"

His suspicious look fires up my own paranoia. Something isn't right here.

"Just go," Layton says, "It's getting late."

"Sure," David murmurs and disappears into the after-work drinking crowd.

"We need to talk," Layton says and gestures with his head for me to follow him.

I follow him cautiously. He's going to tell me that they got jumped on the way home, and that Ruby is in a bad way. That's why she's sleeping. It has to be.

He leads me into a quieter corner near the gents' toilets, where no one wants to stand and socialize unless they have to.

"Look, mate. I'm going to come right out and say this," he says. "Ruby and I had sex in her home tonight. I know that I'm a bastard, you don't have to tell me. I know how you feel about her, but man...there is something about her..."

My stomach twists into a knot so fierce, I feel like I'm going to throw up. "I'm in love with her," I interrupt him.

"You know that. I brought you into her life. How could you do this to me?"

"I know," he says, looking away. That's how I know he feels guilty. He doesn't break eye contact for anything. But it doesn't make up for the pain he has caused me.

"That's why she fired you?" I ask quietly as the pieces slot into place. "She wants to be with you?" I'm dreading the answer, but what else can be the reason?

"Not exactly," he says with a sigh. "It's complicated. I give her what she craves. You don't need to know the details."

"I *need* to know the details, you prick. I want to be with her, you have literally just whisked her out from under me. I told her a few hours ago. I was hoping she would come around. I know there's something between us and you've just fucked that up."

"No," Layton says, shaking his head, his eyes hard. "This was her decision. I tried to put her off, but it turns out she..." He trails off, a look of desire in his eyes that burns my heart.

"Turns out she what?" I grit out.

"She wants what I can give her. She *needs* it. I don't know what her situation is, but she was into the darkness, mate. She isn't the right fit for you." His voice has gone soft, almost pitying.

"The fuck?" I spit out. "How do you know what the right fit is for me?"

"The women you date are...vanilla. Ruby is," he sighs again with that look I want to punch off his face so hard, his nose will come out of the back of his head. "...dark chocolate cherry liqueurs," he finishes up.

I close my eyes briefly. His words have told me everything I needed to know about how Ruby likes it in the sack. She likes it rough. Really rough.

"I can be that for her," I say quietly, thinking about how turned on she got with the bit of knife play in her office. I'm not as into the darkness as Layton is, I know he is into some hardcore shit, but I've dabbled before. The knife play was for her benefit. I wanted to see if it would turn her on and it did. A lot.

"No," Layton says, shaking his head. "Besides, it's all redundant. She isn't into relationships. She doesn't want one. She wants me for what I can give her, that's it."

I take that in. "She told you that?"

"Yeah. We talked. I see why you love her. She is a remarkable woman with views of the world that put mine to shame."

"She stabbed someone earlier. It didn't even affect her." I don't condemn her for it. I applaud her. She is spectacular. I may not know the full ins and outs of her underworld dealings, but I've pieced enough together so that I know enough to be able to help her. The Pangolin was my way of showing her that and it *did* help her.

"It affected her," Layton says softly. "But she has been absolved of it."

I frown at him. "What do you mean *absolved* of it?"

"You wouldn't understand. This is what I'm talking about," he says patiently.

"You know what, *mate*," I growl suddenly. "You are a fucking arsehole. You betrayed my trust. I thought you would keep her safe, instead you took advantage of her when she was vulnerable. It was a dick move; a serious dick move."

He just glares at me but doesn't say anything. Not surprisingly. He hasn't talked this much since before he went into the military. He came back a changed man, and apparently, also a dick. He never used to be this way. We ran in the same crowd at secondary school. Both of us were into sports and popular with the girls. We were friends. But not now. Not after this.

"You can get fucked," I growl and storm off, knowing that I have to find David and get the run down on what the fuck I'm supposed to do 'downstairs'. I've never even been downstairs, let alone worked it. My temper doesn't abate when I find David, talking quickly into the phone, gesticulating wildly.

"Well, fuck you!" he snaps and hangs up. "Ramsey!" he exclaims when he sees me. "I need you…"

"Figured," I say. "If by Andy you mean Watson, yeah, I spoke to him earlier, he's working Perfect Ten's tonight. Where do you need me?"

"You are a god," David says and indicates I should follow him. "Everything okay with Rubes?" he asks casually.

"Yeah, she's good," I say, not wanting to go into the heartache of Layton's betrayal. It fucking sucks, but I'm not out of the game yet. He has given me valuable information on how to get to her. I just need to figure out how to approach this. I will boot Layton out of her life and be the one to take care of her. I think that's what he was getting at. She is such a badass in her everyday life, she wants – needs – someone to be a caregiver in her downtime. It makes perfect sense and is something that I can definitely give her, if she'll let me.

Chapter Ten

Ruby

I rouse from a deep sleep as the alarm buzzes on my phone next to me. I stretch luxuriously on my thousand thread count pure white cotton sheets. Stark naked from my bath earlier, I open my eyes and sit up, turning off the alarm. I feel refreshed, more so than I have for a long time, realizing that I slept for the longest time I have since I started work here as the Black Widow. It was Layton's care for me that did it. He gave me what I'd been craving all day. He punished me, fucked me like a stallion, gave me the aftercare that I so desperately needed and then he bathed me, head to toe, washed my hair, brushed it out and dried it as if he was used to doing this. I find myself oddly envious of the women he has treated with such care before me. But it gave us a chance to talk, to figure this shit out.

Relationship – no.

Arrangement – yes.

He seemed to be into it, so that makes me happy. It means I don't have to find another BDSM club where I can be stalked and betrayed again. I feel more than a little guilty about the way I turned Ramsey down and then leapt on his friend half an hour later. It is cruel and I hope that Layton lets me explain it to him. I doubt it though. He seems to be a man with some sort of honor. He probably went straight to Ramsey and told him. I definitely need to follow that up. It's not that I don't find him crazy attractive, but he's asking too much from me. I can see it in his eyes.

With a sigh, I stand up, walk out of the bedroom and down the corridor, needing coffee now. I cross the darkened sitting room and down another hallway into the huge kitchen. I don't bother with any lights. I can see well enough in the dark and know where everything is kept in precise locations. I wait idly as the kettle boils, and I make a cup of coffee. I didn't have time to set the coffee maker before Layton and I had an encounter to remember. Smiling as the memory of the blood play comes back to me, I pick up my cup and head back through to the sitting room.

I stop dead in my tracks as I see a silhouette of a man sitting in the armchair by the fireplace.

"Who are you?" I ask, placing my cup down on the nearest side table. I don't freak out. I remain completely calm. Freaking out will only make the situation frantic and when chaos ensues, things go wrong.

He doesn't answer.

"What do you want?" I ask, moving closer to him. For some reason, I don't get a threatening vibe from him. I can't explain it, it's odd.

When he opens his mouth and the words tumble from his lips, I freeze, locked into place.

"Your father sent me, Ruby. I'm here to help."

That voice. That accent.

"You!" I hiss, reaching for my knife to ram into his gut, but I don't have it. I curse as I left them in the nightstand drawer last night before my bath. I clench my hand into a fist. "Get out!" I snarl.

He rises, as graceful as a leopard in the darkness and approaches me slowly, doing up the button on his suit jacket. "I know you are angry with me, but I'm not leaving," he says.

"Angry?" I spit out. "Angry? Oh, angry doesn't cover it, you prick. You...stalker! Giselle told me everything. You are fucking deluded if you think you can break into my house in the dead of night and have a reasonable conversation with me."

"Technically, I didn't break in," he says calmly. "No broken windows or doors or alarm panels. You are still perfectly safe. I would never put you in danger. It's the opposite of what I'm here to do."

"Safe?" I say in disbelief. "I am not safe with you. What you did to me earlier was cruel." I back up again now, but not out of fear of him reaching me, but needing to get to the handgun in the sideboard where my coffee is. Illegal in this country, yes, but nowhere near impossible to get hold of if you know the right people and well, I *am* the right people. In a flash, I have the drawer open and I'm aiming the gun between his eyes.

He doesn't even flinch.

I only then become uncomfortably aware that I'm as naked as the day I was born, with scratch marks on my chest from the knife play last night. The marks on my back twinge, knowing that the man standing in front of me inflicted them and walked out on me.

"I know," he says softly. "I had to leave you, Princess. If I hadn't, I would've..."

"Don't call me that!" I screech, going into freak out mode against my will. Seeing him here in my home, my safe space has had a serious mindfuck moment descend on my rational side. My hand wobbles and I curse as he sees it and within a second has disarmed me and is shoving the gun into the back of his pants.

"Dammit!" I curse loudly and drop my hand in disgust at myself. "Would've what?" I ask after a beat.

I hear him draw in a deep breath. "Told you everything and I wasn't ready for that. I didn't mean to break roles with you yesterday. I wanted to ease you into the fact that I was hired to protect you. Being in that position with you wasn't the best time to come clean."

"Really?" I ask sarcastically, "and when *is* the best time to come clean?"

"Now, I suppose," he says with a slight shrug. "As I said, your father sent me. He has had someone watching you since you moved here. But about six months ago, he was careless and got himself killed in action. That's when your father called me."

"You're lying," I snap. "My father, who works in I.T. out of their home in Westchester, doesn't have the means to contact someone like you."

He tilts his head. "Rex may not be in the business anymore, but he still has connections. Ring him if you don't believe me."

I blink. Is he telling the truth? What does he mean about Rex not being in the business anymore? Have I totally missed something pertinent about my parents' life?

"There is no way my father would sanction you to..." I wave my hand around, struggling for once to find the words.

"What? Role play with you?" he asks. "No, that was me. I needed to know everything about you, so I knew how to protect you. I learned you visited Giselle's place, so I inserted myself into your life. I know it was wrong to keep it from you, but I couldn't help myself. I could see the tolls your life was taking on you and I needed to be part of the comfort you sought. Do you understand me, Ruby?"

I bite the inside of my lip to stop myself from dropping to my knees in front of him and begging him to give me the care he neglected to administer earlier.

"Why?" I ask quietly. "Why do you care?"

"I have grown to care about you, Princess," he says. "You may not know that I've been there all this time, but I have. I've been watching out for you, taking care of threats before they reached you. What happened to you in the alley yesterday is entirely my fault. The guilt is eating me up. I neglected you and it distracted you. If I had taken care of you the way I was supposed to, you wouldn't have been caught by surprise." He drops to his knees in front of me, head bowed. "Can you ever forgive me?"

I stare down at him in shock. I back away to the side to get away from him. He is fucking with my head again. I can't let him do it again.

"Get up," I whisper.

He shakes his head. "I failed you twice, and now I need to pay penance."

"I can't deal with this. Not now," I blurt out.

He grabs my hand to stop me from darting off. "You know how to make me pay," he says quietly in that Irish accent that sends a thrill down my spine and makes me go damp despite how upset I still am with him.

I can think of only one way because we are only involved in *one* way. "We're over," I say just as quietly, hoping that is what he is after because if it isn't, I've just made a complete dick out of myself.

He breathes in and nods, even in the dark, I see him wince with a pain that is hard to fake. "I understand, Ruby," he says. "But I'm not going anywhere. Your father hired me to take care of you and I will."

"You keep saying that, but I don't even know your name," I say, shaking my head in irritation. This man is infuriating.

He rises, again with a fluidity that is so sexy I want to crawl up him and kiss him until I can't kiss anymore.

"My name is Declan Gannon," he says, and my blood runs cold with recognition, freezing me on the spot with a fear that doesn't often paralyze me.

Chapter Eleven

Declan

Ruby has frozen to the spot at the mention of my name. I figured she'd know who I am. Or at least, have heard of me. I hate to blow my own trumpet, but I'm kind of notorious inside the dark underbelly of the English criminal system. It's why I'm here in the first place.

Before I can react, she has darted over to the wall and slammed her hand against it, flooding the room in a warm glow that is quite easy on the eyes after all this darkness.

She looks at me, her expression one of fear before she takes in my face and body with a lustful once-over that makes me smile inside. I often get that reaction, but it has never meant as much as it does right now.

She licks her lips. "You're Declan Gannon," she asks.

"I am," I reply.

"You're a fucking ghost," she says, shaking her head. "No one, and I mean *no one* knows what you look like, and you show up here and give me your fucking name..." She appears to be going into a bit of a meltdown. "You fucking killed my friend!" she yells at me suddenly.

"Oh?" I ask. I've killed many people's friends, I'm sure. "Be more specific."

"Derek Slater," I say bitterly. "You shot him in the head from a thousand yards away from the top of the Deansgate Square South Tower."

"Hmm," I murmur, and then say, "Allegedly."

"Fuck you!" she hisses. "He was one of the good ones! He was an ally, he helped me when I first got here. I was devastated when he died, and it was *you*! Then you stand here, brazen as fuck after pretending to care about me and..."

"Whoa, hang on a fucking minute," I snap, pissed off that she dares to assume how I feel. "I do care about you. I've been watching out for you for months. Do you *know* how many people want you dead? Hmm? Do you know how many of the lower warring factions want to take you down? Have you just been walking around assuming you are fucking untouchable, Princess? Because let me tell you a cold, hard truth...you are not. *I've* been the one to keep you safe. Yesterday was a cock up. A massive one on my part and I can assure you it will never happen again. I'm sorry about your friend. Truly, I am, but I'm paid to do a job and I do it. That's all there's is to it. No right. No wrong."

"Oh, how nice for you to live in such a black and white world!" she yells at me.

I shake my head. "This is getting us nowhere," I point out, reaching for her to grab her arm.

She tries to yank her arm back, but I grip it tighter, hurting her.

"Let go!" she snarls like a lioness on the attack.

"Not until you hear me out, Princess," I say.

"Stop calling me that. It hurts every time you say that word."

57

Her genuine upset makes me feel guilty all over again. "I'm sorry for leaving you yesterday. I hate myself for it."

"Good," she says. "I hate you too."

That stings. A lot. My feelings for her are infinite and standing right next to her naked body and not devouring every inch of her, is taking all the willpower I have.

"What can I do to make it up to you?" I ask sincerely.

"You can't. Another man had to come in and do the job for you. How does that make you feel, *Daddy*?"

"Don't provoke me, Princess," I growl, feeling the hit in my nuts as she'd intended.

"Why? What're you gonna do? Whip me and leave again?" She is absolutely furious now; her deep green eyes are flashing with fire. It's turning me on in ways I can't even express. Not being able to touch her, nor have her touch *me*, was something that took an immense amount of strength.

"I should take you over my knee and slap your arse until you scream," I growl.

"What's stopping you then?" she snaps.

I draw in a deep breath and then exhale, calming my temper before I do exactly what I threatened.

And then it happens.

All my rationale falls away and there is only her and me in this room together. I grab her throat, hearing her gasp of surprise, and I shove her up against the wall behind her. I lean in closer, licking her neck, tasting her skin the way I've wanted to for so many months. My cock is pressing up against my pants, painfully erect.

She struggles in my grip, but I don't relent. She turns her head away when I flick my tongue over her jawline.

"Get off me," she growls.

"Not this time," I murmur, squeezing her tighter until she chokes.

Her hands shoot up to mine, clawing at me to loosen my

hold. I don't. I know she is safe. I know the limit. I have strangled men to death with my bare hands before, this is nothing. She knows it's nothing. She is in survival mode and that just makes it even sweeter. I press my other hand to her pussy, feeling her wet my hand, she is so turned on. I palm her gently before I pinch her clit hard, twisting it until she yelps.

"Bad girl," I whisper in her ear. "Stay still for Daddy."

"No!" she chokes out. "Get off me. We are over."

"Not until I say so," I growl.

"You promised," she whimpers as I loosen my hold on her. "It was your penance."

It's like a slap in the face. I stumble back, my heart thumping in my chest. I don't even react when she brings her hand up to slap me hard in the face, her nails out for blood. She gets it. I grunt as she gouges me deeply with those talons, she calls nails. Not long but shaped into sharp points. I see why now.

"Fuck!" I roar, slapping my hand to my cheek. "Jaysus fecking Christ, woman."

She presses her lips together, her shoulders shaking as my usually cultured, lilting Irish accent falls into the rough accent of my upbringing in Finglas, one of Dublin's roughest areas.

"Does that hurt, Daddy?" she purrs, running her hand up my shirt.

I should've known.

I should've been expecting it.

She yanks the handgun out of the back of my pants and presses it to my forehead. "Don't want to shoot you in your pretty face, Daddy, but I will if you touch me again."

"You are cruising for a slapped arse," I growl at her and slap the gun away. She gives me a smile so cruel, so utterly arousing, my lips fall open with a soft pant.

"Promises, promises," she taunts and saunters off,

swinging her slim hips and throwing the gun down on the sofa as she passes.

It's a sign of trust someone in her position will rarely display and it makes me smile wickedly. She is a firecracker, and she has captured my heart, my head and my cock.

"By the way," she calls back. "Seeing as you work for me, we are definitely over, Declan."

Her use of my name, which sounds like honey coming from her lips, pierces my cold heart.

"I don't work for you, I work for your father," I point out, following her through her house to her bedroom.

"Not anymore you don't," she informs me. "You want to keep me safe? You do it on my terms."

"I'll leave it to you to tell Rex then," I mutter.

"Oh, you can fucking count on it," she growls and slams the bedroom door in my face, leaving me on the other side, looking and feeling like a hard cock with no pussy to shove it into.

"Fecking fantastic, darlin'" I mutter and determined to show her I'm not leaving her, not ever again, I stand there prepared to wait however long it takes for her to reopen the door.

Chapter Twelve

Layton

Sipping the hot mug of hot chocolate, I stare out at the breaking of dawn over the city. It's a wonderful view. One I have only learned to appreciate in the last ten minutes, despite living here for several months. Before, my apartment in the exclusive block at no. 1 Castlefield offered mere seclusion and isolation from the outside world. Now I see it as something else. A home of sorts. At the very least, somewhere other than a place to lay my head for the few hours that I can sleep at any one time. Being with Ruby last night was something of a revelation. Women have come and gone in my life. I've never wanted one to stick around for more than a couple of play sessions at best and relationships? What the fuck are they? I couldn't even tell you, seeing as the last time I was in one, was seventeen years ago when I was seventeen years old, and it was more hormones than real feelings. I don't think for a second, or dare to hope, that Ruby wants that from me. She knows what I can give her and that's about the limit to it for her. But for me? Oh, I'm falling for her in a way that has slapped me around the head so fast and so hard, I betrayed my only real friend to be with her.

I sigh and turn from the floor-to-ceiling window as there is a knock at the door. Frowning at it, I approach with caution. Random people cannot just waltz into the building and start knocking on doors.

I open it, mug still in hand, ready to smash into someone's skull if need be. As it turns out, it's a slight, weasley-looking man, who goes by the name of Boomer. No idea why and I don't care.

"What do you want?" I ask.

"I'm here on behalf of my employer," he states in that really creepy monotone which gives away the fact that he is a massive psychopath.

"Okay," I drawl. "What does *he* want?"

"To call in your debt," he says.

The look I give him is definitely one of surprise. "Debt?" I ask. "And what would that be then, mate?"

"You owe him for paying off the man you nearly killed into not pressing charges," he says.

"Oh, do I, now?" I growl, my mood going from dark to black in a split second. "That asshole had it coming, and Scott knows it."

Boomer sniffs delicately, his expression one of boredom. "Regardless of circumstance, Scott is calling in his payment."

"I don't owe him anything," I snarl, gripping my mug so tightly, I'm this close to smashing it in my fist, never mind this prick's head.

"Word is you are now working for Ruby Bellingham," he continues as if I hadn't spoken. "Scott needs you to act as his eyes and ears."

"Excuse me?" I spit out. "You want me to *spy* on her?"

"Scott does, yes."

I grit my teeth. So much for there being no animosity

between them. "Forget it. I'm not some grunt who does dirty work."

I don't tell him that I won't betray Ruby, even if my life depended on it. He will use that against me and her and I won't let that happen.

"How *is* your sister doing after her ordeal? Recovered from the trauma yet?" he asks, sticking the knife into my heart and twisting it all in one go.

"She's fine," I lie, trying not to kill this arsehole where he stands. Truth is, Linda is in a bad way, as is completely expected after what happened to her. I played it down to Ruby, so did Scott as we agreed upon. We had a deal that Scott would take care of the damage I caused that night if I disappeared for a while to let the dust settle. Seems the knobhead has started kicking it up again.

"Hmm," Boomer murmurs. "So. Eyes and ears, or off to prison you go," he adds, almost jovially.

"What does he want to know?" I ask, deciding to play along. I need to keep Ruby safe. Rather me pretending to spy on her than someone who will actually mean her harm.

"Everything," Boomer says with a shrug. "If she blows her nose, he wants the tissue. Are we clear?"

"Very," I grit out.

"Marvelous," he says with a sinister grin. "Our employer will be very happy with this arrangement."

I dislike how that went from *my* employer to *our* in one conversation, but the only thing that matters is keeping Ruby safe.

He hands me a cheap-looking mobile. "Keep in touch," he states and turns to leave before looking back at me. "Don't attempt a double-cross. You've heard what I can do to a person's nervous system."

I nod grimly. Oh, I've heard all right. As far as upper-level gang workers go, he is one of the most notoriously violent,

EVE NEWTON

bordering on sick. Where Scott found him is a mystery no one can solve.

I watch grimly as he walks away, feeling a chill settle on the back of my neck. I have to go to Ruby and inform her of this conversation. Together we can decide then what the fuck to do about it.

All of my guilt over what I did to Ramsey dissipating in the face of a bigger issue, I close the door, place my mug and the burner phone down and pull my mobile out of the back pocket of my jeans.

"Ramsey," I say as soon as he picks up the phone with a very curt, "What?"

He knows I wouldn't ring him right now unless there was something else to talk about except for Ruby. That conversation is over and done with.

"We've got trouble," I say, straight to the point.

Instantly, his attitude changes. "Meet me at Widows in half an hour," he says and hangs up.

I replace my mobile in my pocket and turn to the end table. Pulling out the small drawer, I grab the hunting knife and shove it in the back of my pants. I pride myself on not needing to carry a weapon, but the stakes just got raised and Ruby's life is worth more than my ego.

Chapter Thirteen

Ruby

"I've told you, you don't need to be with me twenty-four seven," I growl as *Declan* follows me around the house, while I get another cup of coffee. I don't offer him one. Fuck that. He can get his own or better yet, fuck off to Starbucks down the road.

"Sorry, you are stuck with me," he growls back.

"Fine," I say, seemingly relenting to his obvious relief. "You can drive me to work, seeing as you are here."

"Fine by me," he snarls and waits impatiently while I continue to get ready.

Ten minutes later, he ushers me to the black Aston Martin on the driveway. Of course he drives a DB9. Why wouldn't he? He has a James Bond air to him, might as well play on it.

We are both silent on the drive into the city. I'm thinking of all the ways I can yell at my dad for firstly, lying to me all these years and secondly, for being an overbearing asshole. It has occurred to me several times in the last hour that Declan could be lying about why he is here, but bringing my dad into it would be a stupid move and he is anything but stupid. It reminds me of what he did to Derek, and I grimace, hunching my shoulders and trying to turn off the feelings that have sprouted since his arrival in my home. I still have that need to please him, which is insane because he is a dick, but there's more...I can't quite get my head around it yet. It's more than just basic attraction.

I shove it aside and glare out of the window.

"I really am sorry about your friend," he says a moment later, startling me out of my thoughts.

I turn to face him. "Yeah, you said that already."

"I didn't mean it then. It was platitude. I can't change what I've done, nor would I, but I want you to know that hurting you makes me feel guilty," he says, with an almost confused shake of his head.

"Why did you kill him?" I ask quietly, ignoring his attempt at remorse.

"I don't know," he says with a shrug.

"Who hired you?"

He sighs. "It doesn't work that way, Ruby and you know it."

"How does my dad know how to contact you?"

"You really don't know?"

"Would I be asking if I did?"

"He used to be in the game, that's all I'm telling you. It's between him and you."

"How old are you?"

"Thirty-six. How old are you? Actually, scrap that. I know it was your birthday yesterday, twenty-six."

"Yeah, you ruined it."

"I know."

"Fuck's sake," I mutter and turn away again. Learning that someone put a hit out on Derek makes my bones ache with cold. I'd thought he was legit. He had no obvious ties to the underworld. He did everything he could to help me start off here.

"Where to?" he asks after an uncomfortable pause.

"Canal Street."

"Whereabouts?"

"Do you know Liberty & Justice?"

"I do."

I nod. This is mine as well. The Banker works out of here and it's Thursday. Meet up day.

Declan pulls up moments later, right outside at this early hour. It's barely 6AM.

"Wait here," I say and get out without waiting for an answer.

I walk straight into the gay bar and wave to Franco the manager as I head on back to the offices.

"Hey," I say, seeing the Banker sitting behind my desk, counting up. "We all good?"

"Everyone except Dalglish," he replies. "He asked if we could give him two more days."

I frown. Dalglish always pays up on time. Why not today? "What did you tell him?"

"That I'd ask the boss."

"Okay," I say. "Fair enough. Call off his protection for the next two days. See if that speeds up his ability to pay this week."

The Banker raises his eyebrow at me, with an approving smirk. "Figured that's what you'd say. It's already done."

"Fantastic. I'm fairly certain Maverick will hone in on him like an ant to sugar as soon as word gets out. He'll pay by the end of today."

"He is in a tricky spot right on the border of what's yours and what's Maverick's. Must be in a bit of a hole not to pay this week."

"Hmm," I murmur and then smile. "Take your cut and

distribute the rest to the street team. Something tells me, shit is going to hit the fan out there today."

"You don't say," he drawls and then laughs loudly. "You are a fun one to work for, you know that?"

"Never hurts to hear it," I say and leave him to it, wanting to get back to Widows to see what went down without proper security downstairs last night. I meant to go back, but for some reason, I crashed after my time with Layton and that was that.

I slip silently back into the idling DB9. Declan looks at me expectantly.

"What?"

"Everything okay?" he asks.

"More than," I reply. "Take me to Black Widows."

"Yes, Ma'am," he mutters.

"Hey, you are the one that insisted on driving me into the city. Don't complain about it now."

"Not complaining," he says, pulling away from the curb.

When he pulls into the parking lot of Widows, I see an unfamiliar, small red car parked up. As Declan parks his car, I stare at it, wondering who it is. I'm not left waiting very long when David jumps out of the passenger side and heads off quickly to the back door of the club. I'm about to get out and join him, when the driver's side door opens and a woman gets out, stunningly attractive, even though she is still dressed in her pj's and fluffy slippers with her dark hair bunched up on top of her head. I watch with interest as she calls to him and he turns around. My jaw drops open as I see her run her hands up his chest and slip something into his jacket pocket before standing on her tip toes to kiss him on the mouth with her fucking tongue.

What the actual fuck?

I guess I had him figured out all wrong. What an idiot. I'd

placed him firmly in the gay camp, but clearly, that was wrong and idiotic of me.

"You okay?" Declan asks, looking over to the kissing couple.

"Yeah," I say. "Just surprised." I pull on the handle of the door, but Declan reacts with lightning speed, leaping out of the vehicle and darting around to open it for me, offering me a hand to help me out of the low-slung sports car.

"Thanks," I say, but don't take it, rather needing to *not* touch him in any way and struggle in my heels to get into a standing position.

I stalk past him and catch up with David, who pauses at the door and holds it open for me.

"Morning," he says with a smile.

"Hey," I reply. I don't get a chance to say anything else as Ramsey and Layton come marching down the corridor, faces dark and grim, gesturing that we follow them into my office.

"What's that about?" I ask.

He shrugs. "Probably going to ask you to choose between them," he replies smartly, grinning at me.

"Fuck off," I mutter and head into my office with David right behind me and Declan silently bringing up the rear.

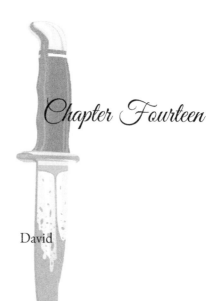

Chapter Fourteen

David

"So who are you?" I ask the silent, gorgeously suited man that drove Ruby to work this morning.

Ruby turns quickly, casting her gaze to him and then to me. "He's no one," she says.

"Declan Gannon," he says, which makes Ruby balk and go slightly pale.

"Seriously," she hisses. "You want all of us to know who you are?"

"I have nothing to hide...well, not from you and..." He waves his hand vaguely at the rest of us clowns that he apparently can't be bothered enough with to learn our names.

"David Jones," I say, and stick out my hand because my mum taught me good manners. Plus, he is uber sexy and those hands are...I can picture them splayed out on Ruby's skin and I shiver.

He takes it with no hesitation and grips it firmly before letting go. I have an urge to lick my hand now.

"I know who you are," he says in an accent to die for. I always did love the Irish. "All of you."

"Hmm," I murmur, wondering who he is really and why Ruby doesn't want us to know his name. Must be something underworld-y. I know stuff because I work for the Black Widow but I'm not part of the actual goings-on and that suits me. Darkness is not my jam. I tune out whatever they're saying now and concentrate on Ruby. Her cheek is battered, and her lip looks sore, but her eyes are lit up like she's had amazing sex followed by a great night's sleep. My eyes drift over to the Irish god and Layton, who is also quite the hottie. Which one? I'm not at all jealous, even though I have been in love with this woman since I came to work for her three years ago. I know she thinks I'm gay, so many people do because of my exuberant nature but that's not the case. I used to be until I realized that I didn't care about gender. I discovered I could be attracted to a person whether they had a cock or a pussy. The little scene outside was meticulously planned by me to show Ruby that I'm not just about the men. Jess, my next-door neighbor was happy to play along. Always up for doing a spot of acting. Now she will see me for who I really am and then hopefully she will fall in love with me. I sigh. That's a joke. She won't even look twice at me when she has these three goons drooling all over her.

"You okay?" Ruby asks, concerned with my huffing.

"Fine," I reply.

"Hm," she murmurs and then looks back at Layton. "Tell me everything."

I tune back into their conversation and then wish I'd been paying attention from the get-go.

"Scott sent his enforcer to blackmail me into spying on you," Layton says, his voice dark and low.

"Wait? What? Scott?" I blurt out.

"Yeah. Not so much an ally," Layton says. "I agreed to play along because rather me than someone else who will actually report back to him on your activities."

"You're going to double cross him?" I ask with a shiver.

"It's the only way to keep her safe. We can sit down every week and decide what information to drip feed him."

"Or I could just shoot him in the face," Declan says.

"Uhm. I agree with Irish, over here," I pipe up. "If we know he's part of the problem, why not take him out?" I find nothing wrong with this sentence now, even though three years ago I'd be appalled by it. But it has shed some light on the Irishman. Killer for hire. No wonder there is no light in his deep blue eyes. He lives in the darkness, a ghost. But Ruby clearly has him wrapped around her fingers. He can't keep his eyes off her. None of them can. Not even me.

I snap my attention back, having drifted off again and smile at her when she looks at me.

"Can we talk?" she asks.

"Sure," I reply and wait as she shoos the other men out, having come to some sort of plan about Scott. I should've known there was something shady about him. He just looks like a creep.

When we are alone in her office, she says, "I owe you an apology."

"What for?" I reply.

"I didn't realize you were... I assumed you were gay and that was wrong. I should've taken the time to find out...to ask about you more."

I chuckle at her obvious floundering. "Don't be a twat," I say. "I'm here for you. I don't expect you to ask about me all the time. I could just as easily tell you things."

"Still. It's very selfish of me. Can you forgive me?"

"Nothing to forgive," I say with a shrug, but search her

eyes, looking for something—anything—to indicate a flicker of interest.

My mouth goes dry when I see it. I wasn't actually expecting it. It's not attraction, or at least I don't think it is. It's hard to tell what she's hiding behind those deep green pools. She is a master of the poker face, but there is something there. A tiny smidgen of... something. I guess only time will tell.

Chapter Fifteen

Ruby

I have no idea what to make of this new side of David. I always thought he was a good-looking man, but not only does he work for me, I assumed he wasn't into women. Kind of wish I hadn't taken him shopping with me for new lingerie a few months ago. Although, I didn't get a vibe from him that he was perving over me. I'm just being silly and vain. Just because he likes women as well, doesn't automatically mean he is into me, for fuck's sake.

I'm almost glad when Ramsey interrupts us. "Can we talk?" he asks.

"Yes," I say gratefully, needing to clear the air about Layton.

"Outside?"

I nod and follow him out, giving David a small smile.

Ramsey opens the back door of the club and props it open.

"I'm guessing Layton told you about what happened last night?" I jump straight in.

"He did," Ramsey says carefully.

"I want to say that I hate the way I brushed you off last night. I was angry and my cheek hurt like fuck. Something had happened prior to me being jumped and I was trying to process, along with everything else, and your declaration came out of the blue. It's no excuse. I should've been more sensitive and please know that being with Layton wasn't any reflection on me trying to hurt you. I needed it and he was there. The upside didn't come until later, as I'm sure he told you..." I pause but he doesn't say anything. Those dark eyes are studying me and he's taking it all in, but he expects more. It's a tactic I usually employ myself. Stay silent, so the other person rambles themselves into a hole they quite often can't dig themselves out of. Still, I need to say it and he needs to hear it.

"I intend to keep him around, but we aren't together. I'm not one for relationships. Not in this life I'm in. They're a liability and anyone close to me can be used against me. Case and point, Layton. Scott got one whiff of a chink in my armor, and he abused it. Do you see where I'm coming from?"

"Yeah," he croaks out. "I know all of this, but I'm still willing to give it a go. I can be what you are looking for Ruby. I can give you the darkness you crave, but it's up to you to realize that now. I won't waste my time trying to convince you with words, but I will show you with my actions. I will be here for you, whatever you need, whenever you need it."

I shake my head. "Ramsey..."

"Don't reject me again, not yet," he says quietly, taking my hand. "If you weren't into this life, would you have me?"

I close my eyes and wish he hadn't asked that question. "I can't answer that. I *am* in this life."

"But if you weren't," he persists.

"Then, yes, probably." I give him what he wants. Only it also seems to also be what I want. The thought of not being with him now suddenly doesn't make sense anymore. "But I don't want darkness from you. I have Layton for that, and that's not really you, is it?"

He raises an eyebrow at my use of present tense. "Then what do you want?" he asks, his voice low and dark.

"Normal," I whisper, staring into his eyes. "As normal as a relationship can be in my world. I want dates and curling up in front of the TV. I want to laugh and cook dinner. I want to take you in a way that the woman inside me cries out for but my darkness squashes. I want to keep you separate from my work. I don't want you to be any part of it."

"But I am. Whether I work upstairs or downstairs, I'm here."

"Then we can never have it," I say sadly.

"Don't," he growls at me, crushing my hand. "Don't fucking do that. Don't give with one hand and take away with the other. I told you I will quit my job, but I can't quit knowing what I know. That's not fair, Ruby and you know it."

"Life isn't fair," I say bitterly and drag my hand out of his.

"No!" he snaps and grabs my arm to stop me from walking away from probably the best thing that will ever happen to the girl I used to be before all of *this*. "I won't let you walk away from this. I love you and I will treat you like a queen. I don't even care about your arrangement with Layton. You can have him how you want him, you can fuck each other in all the ways you need, as long as you come back to me. I need you, Ruby. Don't not start this because you are afraid."

"Afraid?" I balk at the word. "I'm not afraid of anything." Okay, not true. I experienced real fear when Declan told me his name. Not because of him, but because he told me who he was. It's a dangerous game with killer players and knowing the names and faces of assassins in this business is a big liability and he has, inadvertently, or maybe advertently, put me in danger by telling me. In fact, all of us now.

It brings it all home that the five of us are now in this together. Ride or fucking die, by the looks of it.

"Fuck's sake," I mumble, cursing the day I ever set foot in Giselle's. Not that it matters. Declan would've wormed his way into my life somehow and at some point, dragging the rest of us down with him.

"Is that a yes?" Ramsey asks, a soft smirk forming on his lips.

"Yes," I say, the disbelief in my tone evident even to my own ears. "Fucking, yes. But the second you can't handle my arrangement with Layton, you are out. Do you hear me? You go, not him. I don't want to see or hear even a peep of envy or jealousy. That has nothing to do with this. They are separate. And as for you working for me, well, fuck it. If this relationship goes south, you have made it clear that you can find another job, so..." I shrug.

He laughs loudly. "You are priceless, my queen," he says and kisses my hand. "I accept all of your terms and you will not hear a peep out of me about Layton. I promise."

"One more thing," I say before he decides to seal this with a kiss to my lips. "About you working for me. It isn't just about if things go wrong. I need you to trust me to know what I'm doing. You don't interfere with my decisions based on worry that it's too dangerous and you don't jump into the line of fire to save me. I can take care of myself and if it all goes sideways, Declan has my back. *You* are not my personal security. Are we absolutely clear about this, Ramsey? It is one-hundred percent a deal breaker and if you cross over this line, it's the end of us."

His jaw clenches. "I won't apologize for wanting to keep you safe," he says. "I'm not a wilting flower. I know how to fight and I'm not afraid to jump into the middle of a dangerous situation. Hell, it's my fucking job."

"I know that, but this is different. The players are not your average joe who comes into the club for drinks after working in the city in his three-piece suit. They are dangerous and they won't hesitate to kill you. Agree to this or I walk away."

I can see it is going against everything he believes in but if he doesn't do this, then I'm out. I can't be worrying about him. That's the whole goddamn reason I don't get involved with anyone.

I am seconds from backing out of this, knowing it was a huge mistake, when he says, "Fine. You win. I won't be the hero, but know that it will be killing me if I have to stand on the sidelines."

"I respect that and thank you."

He stoops down from over a foot taller and presses his lips to mine softly. "I look forward to where this is going to lead, Ruby Bellingham."

"Same," I murmur and then look over to the open door where there is a soft knock. Declan is standing there, leaning against the door jamb casually.

"You trust me to have your back, Princess?" he asks, a smile playing on his lips.

"Lurk much?" I snap at him. "And stop calling me that."

"No, I don't think I will, Princess. You will come around. I have seen that with my own two eyes this morning." With that, he stalks off, leaving me reeling. Just great, his spying on me has trussed me up like a Christmas turkey. He sees now I will bend in my resolve. Damn him.

Damn him and the horse he rode in on.

Chapter Sixteen

Ruby

I find Declan in my office, staring at the wall, deep in thought. He turns his head when he hears me come in and smiles.

"Do you make a habit of listening in to people's conversations?" I ask, going to sit down behind my desk.

"Always. And I don't just listen, I observe as well."

A shiver goes down my spine and I make a mental note to remember to do a bug-slash-camera sweep when I get home.

"Do you have anything to say about what you heard?"

"I've said all I wanted to about that."

"Good," I murmur and then pounce on the subject that has been plaguing me since yesterday. "What do you have over Giselle Marchand that would make her betray me?"

His face doesn't portray any type of emotion or give me any clue as to what he is thinking. I thought I had an okay poker face, but this man invented it.

"I can help with that," David says, casually slouching against the door frame much like Declan did earlier, plain brown folder in hand. I can't help the teeny tiny thought that he looks really sexy. I berate myself for being a wanton whore. All of a sudden, he has become fair game and it's just my alpha female attitude running amok.

"Oh?" I croak out, earning myself an interested look from Declan.

I clear my throat and hold out my hand. "What have you got?"

"Well, while I don't know what she had for breakfast on the first of July, 1996, I do know that she is in deep trouble financially," he says, pushing off from the doorway and approaching my desk. He hands me the file.

"Oh?" I ask, intrigued. "I thought her club was doing well."

"It is. She is a bit of a spender and well, she is in Scott's territory. He is bleeding her dry every week and she's letting him."

"What?" I snap. I knew she was beholden to Scott's protection racket, but I thought he was fair. All sorts of shit is being dredged up about the asshole I thought was an ally. That's the problem in this business. Everyone has two faces, the one they show you and the other one that will happily stab you in the back with a smile. Even me, I suppose. Although I do try to be more one-faced about the stabbing. Cross me and you get the business end of my blade. Simple. Easy. No delusions.

"Well, 'letting him' is a bit harsh, I guess. She probably doesn't know any better. She seems to be a bit naïve and is just paying what he demands," David amends.

I inhale and think. I want to destroy that bitch, but getting on the wrong side of Scott right now is probably not the best move. But when did I ever let that stop me?

"Find a dummy, make her an offer she can't refuse and buy her out," I state.

"Ruby," Declan warns.

"You heard what I said to Ramsey. Don't make me repeat myself to you," I state, not even looking at him.

"By an offer she can't refuse, you mean..." David makes a slashing motion at his throat.

"Obviously," I snap. "What did you think I meant? More money that she can piss away? No, my intent is to destroy that bitch and make her rue the day she ever crossed me." I'm in a seriously pissed off mood now and the urge to gut someone like a fish is tearing at me. "Declan, you had better speak up now about what you have over her. I'm in no mood to listen to vague bullshit."

"Princess," he says quietly, drawing David's eyes over to him. "Let me soothe that anger."

"Uhm," David stammers and backs out. "I'll leave you two...yeah..." He slams the door shut behind him.

I turn on Declan. "Don't think you have any sway over me now. That ship has sailed."

"I don't think it has. It is still in port and I'm going to make you see that you need me."

"What I need is for you to start talking..."

He grabs my hand and hauls me to my feet. Turning me around, he bends me over the desk without a word. The naughty little girl inside me comes out to play and I don't move a muscle, biting my tongue to stop words from escaping my lips.

I brace myself as his hand smacks my ass so hard, I rock the desk forward with my body, closing my eyes at the relief it brings me.

"Let me touch you, darlin'" he whispers. "Let me touch you in your most intimate places."

"Yes," I murmur, opening my legs so that he can hike my

dress up and pull my panties down to bare my backside to him.

His hand slips in between my legs, cupping my pussy before he drives three fingers into me, making me cry out. He withdraws and moves me over to the corner of the desk, placing me so that the wood is pressing against my clit.

"Use the desk to make yourself come," he whispers. "I want to watch you work for it, Princess."

I gasp at the order, but I won't refuse him. I can't. I am right back where he wants me and well, balls to it all.

I want it too.

Chapter Seventeen

Declan

Pushing my fingers that are wet with her pussy juice into her mouth, to serve as a makeshift gag, I stare deep into her eyes. She is highly aroused but at the same time, as annoyed as fuck with me. I want to kiss her lips and tell her that I love her, but that's not what she is after right now. She drops her eyes and starts to rotate her hips slowly. I stifle the gasp, pulling my fingers out of her mouth. I want to watch this from afar or I'm going to do something that I'll regret. I will ram my cock into her so hard she will scream. There are two reasons why I don't want to do that yet. Firstly, it has to be *her* move. I won't force her into taking me that way, and secondly, she is now involved with not one but two other men. Something tells me that some consent is going to have to be had from all parties before my cock goes anywhere near her. I don't begrudge it. Not one bit when I can make her do *this* for me.

Her eyes are closed. Her hands splayed out on the desk as she rubs her clit against the dark mahogany. She starts to pant, almost as if she is trying to force her orgasm, but it won't work that way. She needs to bring herself to the climax by degrading herself for me. It's the only way she will come down from the frustration and anger she is feeling over Giselle's betrayal, Scott's blackmail of Layton to spy on her and everything else about this life that takes its toll on her soul.

"I can't do it," she sobs suddenly.

"Work that pussy harder, little girl," I murmur.

She speeds up, riding the corner of the desk as it digs into her clit, but fails to give her the relief she is seeking.

"Please," she begs me. "Let me touch myself."

"No. The desk is your only tool. You will stand there until you come for Daddy like a good little Princess."

"Please," she rasps.

I ignore her plea. I am getting way too much out of this display of subservience to help her. My cock is bulging painfully in my pants, and I can't stop myself from touching it. I unzip my pants and pull my cock out, stroking it gently as she fucks the desk, bending her leg and raising it slightly to change the angle for the better. She moans.

"Look at me," I whisper.

She raises her eyes to mine and her lips part when she sees me tugging on myself.

"This is what you are doing to me, Princess," I say in the same low tone as before. "Can you see how much you are turning me on?"

"Yes," she pants. "Yes, Daddy."

My heart thumps as she finally relents and calls me what I so desperately needed her to. I move closer to her, jerking off faster now.

"Ride the desk, baby girl. Come all over it and then Daddy has a special surprise for you."

"Ah," she cries out and circles her hips faster, practically crawling onto the desk to get closer to it so it will get her off.

"You can do it, baby," I pant. "Make me come all over your face."

She scrunches her eyes up and then with a loud moan, the climax washes over her, soaking the wood pressed against her pussy.

"Oh, yes," I groan and allow myself to come all over her face, splashing her closed eyelids and mouth, her battered cheek before I aim the last drops at the wood between her legs. "Now get to your knees and lick it up," I instruct.

She hesitates, but then drops and starts to lap at the wood, cleaning up her mess as my cum drips down her face.

I put my dick away and go to her, stroking her hair as she licks the desk. "There, Princess. You see how happy you've made me?"

"Yes, Daddy," she mutters.

"And don't you feel happier now as well?"

"Yes," she says.

"Stand up and let me hold you."

She rises and turns to me. I wipe her face clean with a hanky I pull out of my pocket before she falls into my embrace, and I stroke her hair. "I will always love you, Princess. You just need to be a good girl."

"I want to be good. I don't want to be bad," she whispers.

"I know. I know." I tangle my fist into her loose hair and pull her head back gently. I brush my mouth over hers, tasting the cum coating her lips. I don't push my tongue into her mouth as much as I want to. She isn't ready for that, yet. She needs to be comfortable with me again. She needs to feel safe and secure that I won't leave her again.

Our moment is broken when the door opens, and David sticks his head in. "So sorry to interrupt," he says, not sounding sorry in the slightest. "The Hot Fuzz is here and, well, you need to get out there and *you*..." He gives me a stern look that makes me want to smile because he is protecting me. "You need to stay in here."

He does a bang-up job of ignoring the fact that Ruby still has her dress up her hips and her knickers down her ankles. He is a treasure that is hard to find. Ruby is lucky to have him. She is lucky to have them all. I just hope that she feels lucky to have me.

Chapter Eighteen

Ruby

Giving Declan a shy smile, I bend to drag my panties back up and shove my dress down. Thankfully, David beat a hasty retreat, after he delivered the news that the cops were here. Well, one cop in particular.

"Excuse me," I murmur and disappear into the bathroom to clean up and make myself look presentable, and not like a dirty whore who engages in filthy behavior in her office at work. I can't help the shiver of delight that goes over me though at actually being that dirty whore. I would never, *could* never debase myself to that level for anyone other than Declan. He does things to my soul that no other man will ever be able to touch.

That is a problem.

A big, massive problem.

I sigh and push this predicament to the side. I have a bigger issue to deal with and there is no getting away from it.

When I come out of the bathroom, Declan isn't there. I sincerely hope he did what David told him to do and stay behind the scenes. I don't need the added stress of trying to explain who he is.

Walking out to the bar area, I plaster a smile on my face. "Detective Inspector," I say. "How are you this morning?"

D.I. Smith turns to look at me. His eyes narrow when he takes in my battered cheek, but then he looks the other way.

Figuratively, of course.

We have a tenuous relationship at best, but for a cut of my illegal earnings, he *helps out* on the rare occasion that I need him to.

Like today.

"Miss Bellingham," he clips out, ignoring my pleasantries. "Do you know anything about the incident in the alley next to this establishment yesterday?"

"What incident?" I ask innocently.

"Apparently a man was set upon and allegedly stabbed before he left the scene of the crime. Ring any bells?"

"None at all," I say, looking him dead in the eye.

He knows I'm lying but he nods anyway. "Would any of your staff have any information?"

"I doubt it. We were all inside yesterday."

"All day?" he asks.

"Yes," I reply.

"Very well. If you or they can think of anything, do give me a call," he says, which translated actually means 'don't ever fucking call me, you psycho bitch.'

I take the big brown envelope that David silently hands me after he appeared like a ghost and hand it to D.I. Smith. "That's all I remember," I say.

He takes the envelope and folds it over, stuffing it into his jacket pocket. "Good day, Miss Bellingham."

I watch him stalk out and exhale in relief, turning to the bar to lean on it for a moment. I feel like it's always a gamble when he shows up whether it will go according to plan or not.

Big, strong arms suddenly wrap around me, and I lean back slightly with a smile as Ramsey kisses the top of my head. "Everything okay?" he asks.

I tense up and frown. "What are you doing?" I ask stiffly.

"Asking if everything is okay," he says cautiously.

"And what does that do?"

"Crosses a line?" he asks.

"Yes, it crosses *the* line. The one I set for you. It's all good. Don't worry about it."

"Ruby," he says with a sigh.

"Go home, you need to sleep," I say, trying to add some warmth to my voice after my icy tone.

"Yeah," he says and turns me to face him. "I'm sorry. It was just a question. I wasn't being an overprotective wanker."

I snort. That word gets me every time. "I know it will take some getting used to."

"I'll head out and see you later," he says, kissing my mouth lightly. I want to devour his lips with mine, but Layton is sitting in the corner so probably not the best time. I wonder if they've spoken about it this morning.

I wave Ramsey off and march straight over to Layton. He has a mug of something in front of him and I sit. "Did Ramsey tell you about us?"

"He did," Layton says.

"Did he also tell you that he is fine with our arrangement?"

"He did."

I nod slowly. "Got anything to add?"

"Nope."

"Didn't think so," I murmur and stand up.

"Wait," he says before I walk away. "I need to keep working for you. Scott expects me to be on that door. If I'm not, he'll know something is up."

"Yeah," I agree. "I know. Are you okay with that?"

89

"Definitely. It means I can keep an eye on you."

I pause and then say, "I told Ramsey that he wasn't to worry about me and jump into the crosshairs. You, on the other hand, may be required to insert yourself into the line of fire."

"Figured. Don't worry about me, sweetheart. I know the score."

"Okay," I say with a smile. "You should probably also head out. I need you back here later."

He nods and picks up his mug. He says, "After I've finished this."

Feeling decidedly better about today after a rocky start, I head back to my office to find Declan has returned and is sitting in my chair, his feet up on the desk as if he owns the place.

"I still think we should just get rid of Scott," he says idly.

"No," I say. "Getting rid of him will open a vacuum that will need filling. The weaker factions will fight for the right to take his place and that will only lead to entropy on the streets. This is *my* city. My home. I will not let a battle break out because I took out one of the bigger gang leaders. His actions haven't reached that point. Not yet. We sit on this until – *if* – it comes to that. Do not, I repeat, *do not* do something rash thinking you are helping."

"You're thinking of the bigger picture," he states. "I get it."

"Do you?" I ask, needing confirmation that he will not go rogue.

"I do. You impress me, Princess."

"I find that extremely insulting, asshole," I growl.

He chuckles and stands up. "Can I see the rest of your operation?"

"Ask David to show you. I have work to do."

He trails his hand slowly down the length of the desk to

the corner of pleasure. "Enjoy your work," he murmurs and saunters out of the office, looking all sexy in his expensive suit. He gives a whole new meaning to tall, *dark* and handsome.

I forget about him and everyone else as I pick up the folder David left on Giselle and get to work reading how far up the river without a paddle she really is.

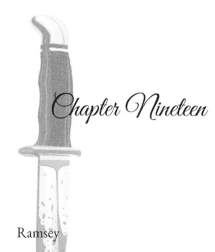

Chapter Nineteen

Ramsey

F eeling the stress of the night draining my energy faster than ten rounds in the ring, I push open the front door of my apartment. Before I can take a step inside, I'm approached from behind swiftly and whacked on the back of my head with something heavy, hard and unforgiving that makes me go down. Dropping to my knees, I groan, putting my hand up to the back of my head, the blood already seeping out of my skull.

"Fuck," I groan and try to stand up, but a cloth is pressed to my face and within seconds my vision goes blurry and then nothing.

"Rise and shine!"

I hear the bright call before cold water hits my face, rousing me to the point of consciousness. I try to move, but my arms and legs feel too heavy to move and my head is aching.

Someone grips my chin tightly and lifts my head up. I struggle to open my eyes, the water dripping into them when I crack them a tiny bit. "You awake?"

I pause. I don't recognize the voice. I try to move again, but this time the bite of plastic digs into my wrists, alerting me to the fact that I'm tied up. I'm upright, which is a plus, but other than that, my situation appears to be dire.

I force my eyes all the way open and try to take in what I can. My vision is gray and hazy, but the face in front of mine is male, which connects with the voice I heard. I'm wet through and cold, shivering in my damp clothes in the middle of what I can barely make out to be an abandoned warehouse.

"He's awake," the man laughs, letting go of my chin and then punching me in the face, snapping my head back by the force of the blow.

"Wrap up, you knob," another voice grates out over my loud grunt of pain.

This fucker has broken my nose, blood is pouring out it. My eyes will start to swell up soon, not that it matters. I can't see for fuck anyway.

I try to wipe the blood away on my shoulder, but I don't succeed much.

"The boss wants him in one piece."

"Why? What does it matter?" the first guy says.

"Because," a voice with a broad Manchester accent pipes up. "We want to show her that we've got him first."

"Jake Noonen," I growl, beyond pissed off with myself for being jumped outside my own apartment by this arsehole's nutters.

"That's right, lad," he says, walking into what would be my view if I could see properly.

"Can't we just start sending him back to her in pieces?" the first guy growls again.

"No!" Jake snarls and the sound of flesh on flesh, followed

93

by a soft grunt tells me that he just got a fist to the face. Can't fault Jake for getting his own hands dirty if the situation calls for it.

"We tell her first, watch her scramble to get her fella back and if it takes too long, *then* you can start cutting off his fingers to send to her. Got it? The idea is to watch her in action. I want to know every move she makes, every contact she gets in touch with, every favor she calls in. Are we clear?"

"Yes, Boss," is the muffled reply. "What's too long?" the second guy asks.

Good fucking question.

"A couple of days or so," Jake replies. "Work him over if you must, but no body parts. It will antagonize her and that's not the purpose of this game."

I wonder what the purpose is. I mean, I know he just said he wanted to see what Ruby will do, but why? What is the reason behind it? It seems odd to me, just a bloke not involved in underworld crap to understand what Jake is trying to achieve here.

"Fine," first guy says with a sigh, which is followed up with a boot to my knee which hurts like fuck and makes me cry out unintentionally. I'm going to rip this guy's face off with my teeth if I ever get out of this. Little prick.

Another punch to the face, which splits my lip and aggravates my busted nose, is then repeated again and again until I can't hold my head up any longer. If I had been in any decent shape to begin with, I'd have put up more of a fight, but they got me when I was tired, ambushed me from behind, knocked me out and tied me up.

"Cowards," I snarl, spitting out a mouthful of blood. "Untie me and see how far you get."

It's big talk, nothing more. If they untied me now and asked me to stand up, I probably couldn't. Still, they don't need to know that.

"You wish, arsehole," the second guy growls at me.

I hear footsteps retreating and figure Jake has taken his leave, which now means these two goons are unsupervised.

I brace myself, expecting the action as soon as one of them grips one of my bound hands tightly.

"Do nails count as body parts?" he growls in my ear and then the howl that echoes through the warehouse makes me sick to my stomach knowing it's mine, as he rips the nail off my thumb, laughing maniacally as I resist the urge to throw up at the white-hot pain that flashes through my hand.

All I can think of as he tears the nail from my index finger is that Ruby was right. They're using me to get to her and I'm a liability.

Part of me hopes she doesn't come for me, leaves me here to show them that she can't be threatened by these pricks, but most of me hopes she comes for me so I can tell her I'm sorry.

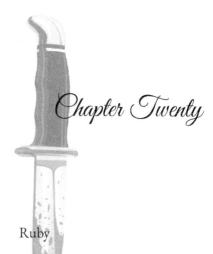

Chapter Twenty

Ruby

A fter an hour, I stretch and lose focus. Even after the best night's sleep I've had in a while, I feel tired and unable to concentrate anymore. My phone beeps for a message in my handbag, but I ignore it as I stand up and stride across the office, dragging the door open. Declan and David are still MIA, so I'm assuming they are downstairs. I head down the corridor to the secret door and slide it open, making sure to shut it behind me. Despite my exhaustion, I have to be here tonight. It's been two nights running that I've not made an appearance and it will only give those who want to force me out, a reason to try. Taking the steps quickly, I pause when I see Declan, David and Layton sitting at the bar, sharing a drink and laughing like old pals.

It surprises me that Declan knows how to laugh. His whole life is filled with darkness and death. I suppose that means he is good at compartmentalizing. Splitting his work from his normal life.

"Hey," David says, waving me over.

I smile and approach them warily. I feel like I'm intruding but the other two men smile and beckon me to come closer.

"Did you know that Irish over here has a Christmas jumper that his mum knitted him, and he wears it every Christmas when he goes back home?" David says.

I look over at the darkly gorgeous assassin and snort laugh. "Really?"

"True story," he says and takes the shot that David hands him.

"And...that tall, devastatingly handsome and pretty brooding, despite his sleek black Merc, also rides a moped?"

I press my lips together, a gleam in my eye as I try not to laugh at the thought of his huge frame on a tiny moped. "Do you go to Brighton a lot?" I snicker, losing the battle.

"As a matter of fact, yes," Layton growls at me and also takes the shot David hands him.

"What about you?" I ask David. "Seems you've managed to get secrets out of these two. What's yours?"

His hazel eyes meet mine and search them heavily, almost causing me to shy away before he says, "No secrets. I am an open book. It's part of my charm."

"Well, no doubt you have that in spades," I murmur, dropping my gaze first, which is totally out of character for me. What the hell?

"And you, Miss Ruby?" he drawls in a bad Southern states of America accent. "What secrets do *you* hold? In fact, one in particular, I'm madly curious about."

"Yeah?" I ask, folding my arms across my chest. "What's that then?"

"How did you get the name the Black Widow?" he asks.

It's like a bullet to my heart. It comes out of nowhere.

I stumble back, tightening my arms in a defense that is useless against the onslaught of memories that flood through me, flashbacks that I can't unsee, trauma that haunts me but that I push away with the darkness that lives inside me. I suppress it most days. I hardly think about it anymore, but the suddenness of David's question...I wasn't ready for it. It caught me unawares and my defenses were down.

"Ruby?" he asks, but his voice sounds really far away.

"Ruby," Declan's soft, lilting voice cuts through the pain. "You don't have to answer that."

I shake my head and back away, falling back into that day as if it was happening all over again.

Eighteen years old and my first boyfriend. I'd been holding onto my virginity until the time felt right. We'd been together for six months, but I still wasn't sure. He was.

One day at my home in New York when my parents and sister were out, he decides that if I'm not giving it up, he is taking it.

I struggle.

I fight.

But I'm too weak.

He slaps me hard, and I stumble back into the counter. He punches me in the face and grabs me. He turns me around and shoves my face into the counter, bruising my cheek. He shoves my skirt up and drags my panties down.

I fight.

I scream.

I struggle.

But I'm too weak.

He holds me down, a hand to the back of my head.

Over my screams I hear him cursing at me. "Stay still, you cock tease. You know you want this."

"No!" I yell, louder.

Someone has to hear me.

They have to.

I cry out as he rips my innocence away.

He tears through my wealthy, sheltered life as if it was nothing.

He takes what he wants despite my tears, despite my pleas.

"Please," I sob.

But it's too late.

I stop struggling.

What's the point now?

I close my eyes, scrunching them shut until the tears stop and a darkness drops over me, disassociating myself from the assault.

My father tried to teach me self-defense. I wish I'd tried harder.

I wish I could remember what he said to do if I was ever attacked from behind. That's what this is. An attack.

Grunting interrupts my thoughts.

I open my eyes, trying to focus.

Panting.

Pain.

Fear.

Bleeding.

Remember.

Remember.

Survival.

Survival.

I close my eyes again and he finishes what he started. I gather every ounce of strength I can find deep within myself and that's when the 'click' happens. It's like a switch and rage descends around me like a black fog.

He lets go of my head, laughing.

He slaps my backside.

"See?" he asks. "Wasn't that good?"

With a roar, I rear back and smash the back of my head into his face. I go dizzy with the force of the blow, but it makes him stumble away from me far enough for me to throw myself over the counter to grab a kitchen knife from the block. I don't even give him a chance to beg for his life. I lunge at him, thrusting the knife deep into his chest.

He stops laughing.

Gurgling.

Falling.

Bleeding.

"You fucking cunt," he growls as he drops to his knees.

I don't hesitate.

There is no more fear.

No more pain.

Just blackness.

I shove him backwards and pull the knife out.

I slam it back into him once more.

Twice.

Three times.

Again and again until I have no more strength left in me.

I slide down the refrigerator, until I can pull my knees up to my chest, my panties still around my ankles, blood staining my hands.

My parents find me like that three hours later, telling me not to say a word to anyone outside of the family, they will fix this.

Fix this.

Weeks later, after I've spoken to a special therapist that my billionaire mom paid to keep quiet about what he heard and who I never see again after that day, my sister comes to me.

"You're strong," she says. "You're like a black widow. You will get through this. I will help you."

Black widow. I know she didn't mean it in a nasty way. She was trying to understand and be supportive, but those two words never left me.

That day shaped who I would become. Fierce, dangerous...deadly.

I will always fight for those who are wronged, even if it means becoming someone who is feared. I will never strike first. I believe in vengeance. You hurt me or someone I care about, I will kill you.

It really is as easy as that.

"Ruby." Declan's voice cuts through my thoughts again.

"Yeah," I say, slightly dazed.

I look into his deep blue eyes and suddenly, everything is clear again. He makes things clear in my head. He is my savior. I sought him out for so long, hurting from the pain of that day, hurting myself for being bad, for being *evil*. He gives me absolution for my sins.

His is my...everything.

"I'm okay," I say, my voice steady but quiet.

I look over to David, feeling Layton's intense gaze on me. "My sister gave it to me," I say with a shrug and leave it at that.

He knows there's more. It's obvious from my meltdown, but he nods and drops it.

He leans over the bar and hands me a shot of tequila, which I take gratefully and down in one gulp.

"Well, I should get back to work," David says, which is apparently Layton's cue to also leave to go home. I give them both a bright smile, but when I turn back to Declan, I crumple.

"How do you know?" I ask, falling against him, feeling his arms go around me and hold me tightly, giving me comfort.

"I know everything about you, Ruby. You don't ever have to be afraid of your darkness with me. I understand it."

I nod silently and inhale deeply.

When I exhale, I'm strong again.

I'm about to brush this whole thing back under the mental mat where it belongs, when David comes rushing back into the casino.

"Jake's got Ramsey!" he shouts down to us from the top of the stairs.

The blood drains from my face as the words sink in and then the black fog drops over me again.

No one hurts those I care about and lives.

It's time to end this.

Chapter Twenty-One

Ruby

"Tell me everything," I snap at David, who comes down the stairs, clutching my phone to his chest.

"I don't know anything except that," he says as I meet him halfway.

Layton comes storming back into the casino, having only made it to the door before David announced his news.

"Show me," I say, snatching for my phone.

He holds it up above his head so I can't reach it. "Nope," he says. "You don't want to see this."

"What is it?" I ask quietly. "Is he dead?"

David shakes his head and then jumps as the much taller Layton grabs it out of his hand. "Dammit, you giant," he grouses.

Layton glares at the phone and then hands it back to David. "You don't have to see that," he confirms.

"Give me the phone," I grit out.

David relents under my steely glare and quickly flashes me

the screen before he clutches it to his chest again. It was enough.

Ramsey tied up, beaten and tortured.

"Fuck!" I roar and spin on my heel, hand to my head. I push the emotion aside. I can't let the sick feeling in the pit of my stomach slow me down or Ramsey will die there. I can't fall apart. He needs me to be...*me*. "Where is he?"

"I don't know," he starts.

"FIND OUT!" I bellow and march towards the end of the bar where it sits up against the wall.

"I can find out," Declan says calmly. "Give me a minute."

He pulls out his phone and dials. He starts to talk almost immediately in a language I don't understand, but could possibly be Gaelic? Who knows? Who cares? I need to get to Ramsey.

I stick my hand under the bar, directly onto the hand scanner that sits on the underside. It scans my handprint and opens up an optical scanner in the wall. I place my right eye in front of the scanner, and it scans it. I blink and it does it again. It's highly sophisticated. The blink is imperative. It's a safety precaution so that no one can gouge my eye out in order to open it. I have to be alive and willing to blink. Good luck with that.

It's all for a very good reason. When the door pops open a fraction, I drag it further and slip inside the humongous safe built into the wall. Inside is all of my illegal dealings in firearms, laundered cash, weapons of all kinds and pretty much anything else I don't want the cops to find.

I bend down and grab a black holdall from under the bottom shelf. I open it and then turn to the wall where row upon row of handguns are on display. I start at the top and start to shove weapons into the bag. Guns, knives, flashbangs, a taser, a sword or two. I don't know what I'm walking into, and I need to be prepared.

"Ruby," Declan says from behind me. "What are you doing?"

"Arming up. What does it look like?" I snarl.

"You are not going in there to rescue him. I am," Declan says with a tone that he probably thinks means the end of it.

Yeah, no.

He doesn't tell me what to do. No one does.

"Where am I going?" I ask, ignoring him.

"It'll take some time, but we'll find him," he replies.

I turn on him, pulling my Pangolin out from under my dress to press at his throat. "If you already know and are trying to stall me so you can swoop in and be the hero, you clearly don't know me as well as you think you do. Tell me where he is." I dig the blade into his neck.

He holds his hands up, but there is no panic, no fear on his face. In fact, he is aroused.

The fucker. How am I supposed to be all menacing when he is sporting a hard-on at my best attempt without actually hurting him?

"I don't already know," he murmurs, reaching out to grab my wrist slowly. He lowers the blade and I let him before I tense up and surprise him with my strength. Everyone takes it for granted that I'm a weak, little woman. They don't know the lengths I go to keep in shape. Usually up at 3AM to work out, train for two hours, this has been lacking the last morning due to this asshole currently in my way. Doesn't mean I don't know what I'm doing. After that day, no one and I mean *no one* touches me without my permission or they face the wrath of the Black Widow. I've already stabbed someone this week. Two won't faze me.

"Whoa, okay, tiger," he growls at me as I dig in harder with the blade. "Forgot who I was dealing with," he adds quietly.

"Where is he?" I grit out.

"I honestly don't know...yet," he says with a sigh. "But I will, and then *I* am going in. This is what I'm here for."

"No. You are here to have my back. *I* am here to take care of business. Jake thinks he can fuck with me by taking my boyfriend of an hour, then he has seriously underestimated me." I drop the knife and turn back to my bag to throw more stuff into it. I kick off my shoes and reach around to unzip my dress. I slide the zipper down, but hands overtake mine and do it for me.

"Now, Princess?" Declan asks with a soft laugh.

"Fuck you," I snap and turn when my dress falls to the floor. I take a moment, a quick, vain moment to see if David is looking at me.

He is.

He can't take his eyes off me.

Good.

That's good.

I bend down and pull out some black leather pants, a black long-sleeved t-shirt and a black leather vest from a drawer, along with some lightweight, but sturdy black boots that come up to my knee. Maximum protection without going in weighed down by TAC gear. It won't stop a bullet, but it will slow down a blade.

I remove my thigh holsters and get dressed methodically while the three men watch me silently, then I strap the holsters back on, shove a black hunting knife in the top of my left boot and then zip up the bag. I haul it up, knowing how heavy it is and compensating my balance for the extra weight.

I brush past Declan and say, "Tell me the second you know where he is. That's an order."

"Yes, Ma'am," he murmurs and follows me out of the safe, slamming the door closed behind him.

Chapter Twenty-Two

Layton

The three of us silently watch Ruby leave the casino, heading up the stairs to the main floor.

I turn to Declan as soon as the door shuts behind her. "Do you know where he is?"

"Yes," Declan says straight away.

"What?" David snaps. "You *know* she is going to kill you."

"She can try," he says, completely unconcerned.

"How did you find out so quickly?" David asks.

"I have eyes in this city. Ruby lives here. I'm not leaving a corner of it unwatched," Declan says. "Ramsey is...new...I hadn't gotten around to informing my men that they needed to keep an eye on him. On any of you, really."

I scowl at him. "I don't need protection."

"I bet Ramsey thought that as well," he points out reasonably.

It's hard to argue with that. Ramsey is not an easy man to take down.

"Fair enough," I concede, knowing which battle to pick. "But what about Ruby? We can't let her go into the storm."

"She is the storm," David says with more than a slice of admiration.

"You love her," I say, surprised why I didn't see it before now.

He shrugs, avoiding my gaze. It's hard not to notice Declan's interest in his non-answer.

"Speaking of which," Declan says, clearing his throat. "I'm aware that you and Ruby have entered into an arrangement. I also have an interest in her and while we have been in each other's lives for a while now, I feel it is my responsibility to seek out your consent to be with her on a more basic level."

"Excuse me?" I practically splutter. "Why are you involving me in this? You should be asking Ramsey for his permission, not mine."

"Oh, I'm not asking for permission," he mutters darkly. "I'm interested in a confirmation of your acceptance. If you don't like it, tough fucking luck."

"Humph," I mutter. "You have my blessing."

"Erm," David interjects. "You can't be seriously talking about her like she is a possession."

"Who was?" Declan replies before I can.

But we have massively gotten off topic.

"Where is he?"

"In an abandoned warehouse outside of the city. He is alive and will stay that way. The aim isn't to kill him or even hurt him, despite the evidence to the contrary. He is bait. Nothing more."

I give him a suspicious look. "How do you know that?"

He purses his lips and hesitates to speak. When he does, it

comes as a bit of a surprise. "I have someone working for Jake. A double-cross, exactly for situations like this."

"You need to tell her where he is," David says.

"I will, after the rest of my team have converged on the warehouse and she has more back up than she will know what to do with."

"You mean we're going to let her go in there?" I snarl. "Not a chance."

"But we have to. You saw her. She won't settle for anything less. It's in her nature to save. She has to do this. Do I like it? Hell no, but we have no option. Besides, Jake wants to see what she will do. Once he sees that she doesn't cower behind the likes of me and you, he will think twice about coming for her again in a hurry."

"I don't like this," David says. "It reeks of subterfuge."

"Declan's right. We have to let her go." I hate saying it. I hate thinking about her going in there alone.

"I know that," David says as if I'm stupid. "I was the one who said, 'she is the storm', remember?" He huffs out. "I don't like that we're now all lying to her about..." He waves his hand at Declan.

"It has to be this way," Declan says. "Her father wants her protected and she will not let him go to such lengths. It has to be kept quiet."

"Her father?" David asks. "Which one?"

"Rex," Declan says. "We go way back."

"Interesting," David murmurs.

I take all of this in. I'm curious as to how Ruby's father knows a man like Declan Gannon. It is plain to see from his cold eyes that he isn't just a regular old bodyguard. There's a darkness to him that matches Ruby's, that matches mine. We are three alike and it's slightly unnerving. I pride myself on being a solo player. I don't like teams. Never have. Yet here I am going along with what someone else is dictating. All for a woman who only wants me to choke her while I fuck her painfully hard.

Why is that?

Because you, too, are falling in love with her. After just one day.

I sigh. "I'll do this however you want to play it. You know the score and I want to keep Ruby safe. Where do you want me?"

"At her back," Declan says. "My men are there in case it goes sideways and by that, I mean she gets captured or goes down hard."

"Are we going to let her kill Jake?" David asks quietly.

"We aren't going to let her do anything," I state. "She calls the shots, we're just the backup."

"Precisely," Declan says. "We are getting on the same page."

"You should stay here, though," I say to David to his relief.

"Oh, thank fuck," he breathes out. "I'm not a fighter. But I'll be here providing moral support."

"And it's where you are needed," I say, my hand going to his shoulder. "She'll need you to lean on when we get back."

He nods and scampers off up the stairs.

"Give it twenty minutes and then I'll tell her. Don't worry about your friend. *My* friend won't let him come to too much harm."

I grimace. From the picture that Jake's men sent, it appears that Ramsey is being tortured. I have a terrible feeling that if Ruby ever finds out we stood around here with our thumbs up our arses while her *boyfriend* — yeah, that hurt to hear — gets tortured, she will never forgive us. I don't think it's high on her list of virtues. Cross her once and you'll regret it. That's definitely her motto. I nod and make a mental note to tell Ruby as soon as all of this is over that I want more from her than just sex. She has brought a ray of light to my existence. Even though she is filled with darkness, her smile brightens up a room. Her sassy attitude is a breath of fresh air for me. I want to be everything she needs me for, but I *need* more from her. Hopefully she will come out of this attack unscathed and then we can be together, even if that means being in this with Ramsey and whatever the hell it is she's doing with Declan.

I head up the stairs to find Ruby in her office, a knife held to some man's throat.

Chapter Twenty-Three

Ruby

I loom over the asshole I slammed into my office chair a moment ago. He is small, looks like a weasel and definitely ready to piss his pants scared. My switchblade is pressed at this throat and I'm itching to do some damage.

Layton appears in the office doorway, but I ignore him. He leans up against the doorframe, arms folded, and his mouth shut.

"Who are you?" I ask the weasel, "and why are you snooping around my office?"

He holds his hands up, his answer surprising me. "Dalglish," he says. "Jimmy Dalglish."

I narrow my eyes, recognizing his name as the non-payer from this morning. "Oh?" I ask, easing up on the knife at this neck. "What do you want?"

"I came to ask if you would give me my protection back," he stammers.

"Sure, if you pay what you owe," I inform him.

His shoulders sag. "I can't until the day after tomorrow. Shit is bad this week..."

"Yeah, tell me about it," I mutter, thinking that my own week has sucked balls so far.

"Please," he begs. "I will pay with interest if you can just get Maverick's boys off my back. They smashed in my shop window."

"Sadly, not my problem," I say, not feeling guilty. "You see, the thing is...if you don't pay me, how do I pay my team? Do you see my dilemma, Jimmy? I'm not going out of pocket for you, when I have no guarantee that you'll pay up the day after tomorrow."

"I will! I swear!" he says, looking over his shoulder at Layton, clearly hoping for a different answer.

It pisses me off. *I'm* the one in charge. Why does he assume Layton has anything to do with this?

"Don't look at me," Layton says with a shrug. "This is between you and her."

I grimace, irrationally pissed off with him.

"No can do," I snarl, pressing the knife back to his neck, "and if I catch you sneaking around here again, it won't just be your shop window that I smash in. Are we clear?"

His eyes go round like saucers as he nods. I fall back and let him scamper out of the office. I sigh and then with a roar of frustration, spin and slam the knife into the desk. It reverberates through my arm, so I let it go, watching as it vibrates until it stops.

"Hey," Layton says, coming up behind me. "Come and sit down."

I like that he didn't give me a stupid, useless platitude like 'we'll get him back,' or 'he'll be okay'. He *isn't* okay. He is hurt and it's all my fault for letting him get as close to me as he did. Damn him.

I let Layton lead me to the small sofa in the corner of my office. He sits down, taking up most of the tiny two-seater with his bulk. I raise my eyebrow at him, but he grins and pulls me onto his lap. I giggle, despite the shit situation surrounding me. He wraps his arms around me, and I let him cuddle me.

I let him because it feels good.

It feels nice and comforting to be taken care of when I haven't done anything to deserve it.

"Thanks," I mutter.

"What for?"

"Being here."

We both go silent and then the door bursts open and Declan strides in. He comes up short when he sees me on Layton's lap, but his face doesn't betray any emotion, so I have no idea what he thinks about this.

"Did you find him?" I ask, leaping off Layton's lap.

"Yes," he says. "Let's go."

I nod and clamp my hand around the switchblade handle. I yank it out of the desk and flick the blade back in. Sliding it into the holster, I bend to pick up my bag.

Declan turns and leads the way out of the office with me close behind him and Layton at my back. I don't bother asking where Ramsey is. I don't care. All I care about is getting to him and appeasing the burning hunger I have for hurting those who abducted him.

David is waiting in the corridor, looking anxious. As we pass him, I pause and let caution fly in the wind.

I grab his tie and pull him closer to me, planting a kiss on those sexy lips to his utmost surprise. I let him go and ask, "Do I have a fluffy-slipper wearing skank in my way?"

He snorts with amusement. "The fluffy-slipper wearing skank is definitely *not* in your way."

"Good," I say with a smile and let him go. "We'll talk when I get back."

"I'll be here," he says and steps back with a smile I want to call smug, on his face. "Don't do anything stupid."

"You know me," I call back as we head out to the bar.

"Yeah, I do," I hear him mutter, but ignore the comment.

I know what I'm doing and now...I want it done.

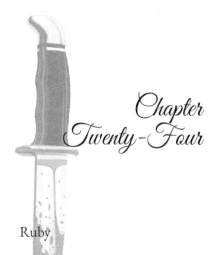

Chapter
Twenty-Four

Ruby

I barely notice the drive out to the edge of the city in the drizzle, in a car that Declan is driving but isn't his DB9. It appeared out of nowhere in the parking lot at the back of the bar, a huge black SUV. Like, hello? How conspicuously gangster of us.

But who cares? All I want now is to get Ramsey back and to make Jake pay for this.

When Declan pulls up outside an abandoned warehouse on a deserted industrial estate, I breathe a sigh of relief. At least we won't attract too much attention.

I climb out wordlessly from the back seat and grab my bag. I unzip it and pull out a handgun, shoving it into the back of my leather pants. I place another on the seat of the car while I pull out two flashbangs.

Shoving one of them down my top to save up my hands for the other one and the gun, I turn and march off towards the warehouse. I don't give a rat's ass that Declan hisses at me to stay put while he does recon. We don't have time for that. *I* don't have time for that.

If Jake seriously wanted me dead, I'd be dead. The attack in the alleyway was a scare tactic, and taking Ramsey was his way of saying he knows who he is to me, that he's watching us closely.

Inhaling deeply, I brush the rain out of my face, glad I had the foresight to tie my hair up in a bun so it's not sticking to my face. I step inside the darkened warehouse on high alert. It stinks of damp, making my stomach clench in protest.

My adrenaline spiking, I shut the door and stick to the wall as I walk around. I can't see anyone yet, just a big open space. My heart is thumping. I'm not afraid, but I am cautious. I have no idea what I'm walking into. How many men are there? What weapons do they have? Is Ramsey still alive? Will they kill him before I get a chance to rescue him? All of these questions are clouding my brain and I need to clear it, or I am no use to anyone.

With my breathing as steady as I can make it, my hands sweating only slightly, I push off from the metal wall and stalk quietly over to the sectioned off offices at the back. I pull the plug on the first flashbang and chuck it straight forward, through the open door, diving for cover with my eyes scrunched shut and my hands over my ears, still holding the gun. Even through the obscene noise of the flashbang, I hear the cries of the several men that it affected. Ramsey is probably one of them, but I can't think about that now. I have seconds to remobilize and get into the offices where I know they now are.

Standing up straight and ignoring the buzz in my ears, I walk steadily over to the doorway, gun leveled, ready to fire at the first person who comes at me. Turns out, it's two, both at the same time, lunging towards me, knives held out.

The saying about bringing knives to a gunfight echoes through my head and makes me laugh out loud like a maniac.

It echoes throughout the empty warehouse.

I plant my feet, aim and pull the trigger.

The noise the shot makes, hurts my ears, but I stand still.

I hit my target in the shoulder, right where I was aiming for. Fatal gunshots are not an option. Not unless it's my life for theirs and right now, they aren't that big of a threat. It's not that I'm scared of killing, it's just a bigger mess to clean up.

"Fuck!" My victim yells, dropping to the ground, hand on his wound, dropping his knife in the process. "You bitch!"

It gives his partner pause. That tells me one thing.

They aren't Jake's best men. They are here as dummy protection. Jake isn't risking his real deals. I wonder why. What is all of this about?

I point the gun at the other man's head.

He practically shits himself, holding his hands up as if this was a stick up.

I almost sigh with disappointment.

That is until my heightened senses pick up movement behind me and I duck the second before someone takes a swipe at my head with a baseball bat.

"Fuck!" I roar and spin in my crouched position to face my attacker. I'm pissed off now. I have no idea where Ramsey is and now, I've got this asshole to contend with. I aim the gun again, but he doesn't even flinch.

It gets kicked out of my hand moments later by the second guy who grew a pair now that the heavy lifter is here.

That's when I fall into a quiet calm. I pull the second gun from out of the back of my pants and stand up. "Where the fuck is he?" I growl.

"You come alone?" my attacker growls back.

"Does it look like there's anyone else here?"

"You've got balls," he says with a laugh, swinging his bat. "You going to shoot me?"

"Yep," I say and aim at his knee. Pulling the trigger and taking great delight in hearing him scream. "I'll ask you again... where is Ramsey?"

I don't think he heard me over his own screams.

I don't bother asking again. They clearly didn't expect me or illegal weapons. I grab the gun that was kicked out of my hand and stalk out of the office. I run up the stairs to the second floor which, consists of sectioned off spaces down the one side.

My instinct is to call out for Ramsey, but I keep as quiet as I can, searching through three of the sections before I find him, slumped in a chair, half-conscious, his arm at an odd angle, his hand messed up where his nails have been pulled off.

I feel the nausea roll over me before I push it back.

"Ramsey," I say quietly, approaching him carefully.

He lifts his head up. "Ruby," he says hoarsely through split lips.

I check the rest of the section to find it's empty. I shove both guns into the back of my pants again and pull out my hunting knife. I go behind him and cut the zip tie that's holding his hands together. He groans in agony which tells me he has a dislocated shoulder and probably a broken wrist as well.

"Can you stand?" I ask.

He nods and stands up straight away, swaying slightly and then grunting, holding his side.

Broken ribs.

"We need to get out of here," I mutter, although I'm still surprised by the lack of real resistance. Something is off, very, very off.

I grab his arm and lead him to the stairs. We take them slowly but as soon as we get to the bottom, Ramsey's knees give away. Distracted, I catch him before he falls and that's when I'm jerked back by a strong hand on my arm.

"You think you can shoot me and walk away?" the guy I shot in the knee bellows in my ear, spinning me around, so that I have to let go of Ramsey, or risk him collapsing into my attacker. Ramsey goes down as my attacker grabs my wrist, the one with the knife in my hand, turning me and viciously dragging it behind my back.

"Ah," I cry out as I feel my arm about to give way, but there isn't a chance in hell, he is getting the better of me.

I kick out, slamming my foot into his shot knee. He screams, but doesn't let go of me. He has a high pain threshold and I'm marginally impressed.

"Bitch," he snarls.

"Been called worse by better," I spit out, knowing I have to get to one of the guns before he does.

Too late. I feel it pressed to my temple and my heart stops for a second.

Just a second.

If this fuckhead thinks he can take me out with my own weapon, he is seriously deluded.

"Ruby! No, this isn't...don't..." I hear Ramsey shout out, but I focus solely on the man holding my arm behind my back and a gun to my head. I have one chance to get this right.

One.

If I miss, or don't hit him hard enough, I'm dead and so is Ramsey. I have no doubt this one will pull the trigger, damning the consequences.

I close my eyes, pushing the scene of the last time I had to do this out of my head. I rear back and as hard as I can slam the back of my head into his nose. He bellows and lets go of my twisted arm. I cry out as it drops loosely to my side, knowing that I've damaged myself by forcing my body into an unnatural angle to headbutt him as hard as I could.

He stumbles back, one hand to his nose, the other waving the gun about wildly. He fires at random, but I'm too late to move out of the way.

The bullet grazes my thigh, tearing through the leather pants and my skin closer than I'd have liked.

"Damn you," I grunt and pull the other gun out, aiming it at his head. The sweat from the last few minutes dripping down my forehead, my ears ringing from the sound of the shot at close range.

All I can hear is my heartbeat.

All I can smell is my own blood.

I tune out Ramsey calling my name.

I flinch when another gunshot rings out and my attacker falls to the floor at my feet, a bullet in his head.

Chapter
Twenty-Five

Declan

"Y"ou absolute fucker," Ruby hisses at me, hobbling over to help Ramsey up.

She's been hit in the thigh, but it hasn't slowed her down.

"He was mine."

"Too bad," I hiss back, grabbing her arm and helping her to move forward.

She drags her arm back and fixes me with a glare so fierce, I fall in love with her all over again. It's not hard. I've loved her since the first time I laid eyes on her back in New York when her father first assigned me to watch her when she was eighteen. Right after the incident that made her who she is today. I hate that I wasn't there for her then, but I can be now, and she needs to know that she isn't alone.

Not anymore.

I will never leave her alone ever again.

I pull her back, probably rougher than I anticipated and sweep her up into my arms. She growls at me, her eyes flashing, but I give her a bright smile that seems to melt her cold heart.

"Sorry, Princess, but you are not walking out of here."

"Damn you," she says, struggling in my grasp, but she is weakened by the rush of adrenaline and the blood loss that isn't severe but is enough to cause me concern. However, we need to move. We have to get out of here immediately.

Layton silently takes charge of helping Ramsey to the door, while I carry Ruby out to the waiting vehicle.

"Wait," she says. "What about him?" She indicates with her head back to the warehouse.

"Not a problem," I say and place her down, popping the boot of the SUV rummaging around in my own bag of tricks.

"You're going to blow it?" she asks.

"Wait," Ramsey says. "What about everyone inside?"

"The two who aren't dead will have scarpered the second Ruby's back was turned," I point out.

Ruby nods in agreement. "We have to get rid of the DB, as well as our involvement. If the other two haven't left already they will as soon as this place lights up. Grenade?" she asks.

I shake my head. "Smacks too much of terrorism. Adds an extra layer of filth. We do this the old-fashioned way." She gives me a searching look, but I'm not revealing my misspent youth to her right now. Maybe one day. I haul a bottle of cheap vodka out of the bag and hand it to her. "Do you want the honors?"

"Oh, you bet I do," she says darkly and takes it, holding her hand out for the ignitor. I hand her a cloth which she douses in the vodka and then stuffs it into the top of the bottle. I hand her a lighter and she turns back to the warehouse.

"Get in," I say. "We'll make it a drive by."

She snorts and nods, climbing into the SUV front passenger side while Layton helps Ramsey into the back. I climb in and circle the car back around. I open the sunroof and she giggles. She stands up and sticks her head and body through the opening, so she can throw the lit bottle straight through the open door of the warehouse.

I look up at her and with a grin of pure delight, she flicks the Zippo open and lights it, holding the open flame to the alcohol doused cloth. She gets her gun ready and throws the bottle. We watch it sail through the air and she aims and fires, hitting the target with an accuracy that my sniper's eye appreciates. She quickly sits back down, favoring her injured leg and I slam on the accelerator and speed off as the warehouse goes up in a burst of flames, burning away any evidence of us, albeit leaving a dead burning body in the middle of it. D.I. Smith will have his work cut out for him, but at least Ruby will be safe.

I pull off my dark gray tie and hand it to her.

"Thanks," she mutters, dropping the gun in the footwell and wrapping the tie around her wound.

I give her a concerned look, but she brushes it off. "I'm fine," she says.

I nod accepting that. I know she is harder than she looks, but I have to trust that she would ask for help if she needed it.

"We need to switch out," I murmur and head to the overpass where one of my men, someone I know from the old neighborhood, has left a uniform hatchback that looks like a thousand other cars in this city. We pile out of the SUV and into the sedan. The SUV will be taken care of.

"Where to?" I ask, knowing she will say her home, but needing to give her that control.

"Home," she says straight away. "I'll give David a call. He can meet us there."

I nod and hand her my phone and tune out her muttered voice as I focus on the task at hand. I can't let my worry for her cloud any aspect of this mission. I need to get us to her home without suspicion or giving anyone any reason to question who we are and where we are going. Speeding, or dangerous driving is out. Slow and steady, watching out for anyone following us.

"Ruby," Ramsey rasps when she hangs up the phone and places it in between us. "You shouldn't have come."

She turns to look at him. "Of course I was coming," she scoffs. "What do you take me for?"

"No, you don't understand. This wasn't about me. It was about *you*. Jake wanted to know every move you made. He wanted to know who you'd bring in... Now he knows."

I glance at Ruby before I look back at the road.

It's not the end of the world. Going in herself will serve in her favor here. But Layton and I will have been clocked as back up, not to mention the half a dozen other men that had the building surrounded in case things went very wrong. I pause in my thoughts and reconsider my original stance. This is bad. Really bad. He knows she goes in headfirst and now he is going to draw her out.

"Give your dad a ring," I murmur as we pull up into her driveway.

"What for?" she asks carefully. "And which one?"

"Rex," I reply. "Just do it."

She nods and picks up my phone again, holding it out for me to unlock, at the same time as she punches in the code to open the huge electric gates.

I drive forward and spot the huge black car already parked up at the same time as she does.

"Dad?" she asks, opening the door before I've come to a stop. "What the hell are you doing here?"

Chapter
Twenty-Six

David

After hanging up the phone with Ruby, I grab my bag, along with her briefcase and handbag, slipping her phone into the side pocket of the bag. I head for the back door and dial Beth. She picks up after four rings.

"Yeah?" she answers groggily.

"Sorry, babe. I know it's early for you, but I really need you in here as soon as you can get in," I say brightly, knowing she is going to bite my head off.

"Ugh!" she spits out. "I've been asleep for two minutes."

"I know, I know," I console. "But Ruby and I have to step out and she trusts you..." I let that compliment hang there.

Beth sighs. "Fine. But It'll be a few hours."

"That's fine, just as soon as you can get here. Byeeeee," I chirp and hang up. Immediately, my sunny disposition fades. Ruby sounded in pain, which means she was injured. But she is alive, and all that matters is that I get to her as soon as possible.

First, I go to the front door and lock it, and then I head

out the back, locking that up behind me and unlocking my phone to call a taxi. I turn and jump a mile when my path is blocked by a large man in a black coat.

"David?" he growls.

"Uhm, who wants to know?" I ask, pressing myself back into the door.

"Come with me."

"No, that's fine," I say. "I'm good."

"I have instructions to pick you up and deliver you to my boss."

"What?" I ask, my voice going higher. If I'm headed the same way as Ramsey, I won't hold up as well. I'll fold like a cheap suit, and I don't do cheap fabric. Gross.

The bear of a man sighs. "Declan sent me."

"Ooh," I say, but then decide I'm not falling for it. Just because he says so, doesn't mean he is telling the truth. "One moment, please." I hold my hand up, turn my back and dial quickly, the first number that comes up.

"What?" Layton growls into the phone.

I glare at it in annoyance. Why is everyone so fucking rude today?

"I need to speak to Declan," I say just as rudely.

Layton snorts, knowing what he did wrong. "He's a bit tied up, right now," he says, badly suppressing a laugh.

I pause. Does he mean that literally? I wouldn't put it past Ruby. I know she's into some fun stuff. I'm sure binding the scary assassin man would be very fun for her. Kind of fun for me too. "I *need* to speak to him," I say again, trying to stress how important it is.

"Everything okay?" he asks, suddenly going serious.

"Did he send someone to come and get me?"

"Hang on." I tap my foot impatiently, as I hear Layton's muffled shout to Declan. I turn slightly and grimace at the man hovering at my back.

"That's Aidan...apparently," Layton says a moment later.

"Wonderful," I mutter and hang up. I turn back to the bear and ask, "What's your name?"

"Aidan," he replies.

"How do you know Declan?"

He just blinks at me.

I sigh and say, "Fine, let's go." I have to trust that this guy is the same Aidan that Declan sent. Otherwise, it's too much of a coincidence for me.

He stomps off to a boring-looking sedan and gets in the driver's side, leaving me to climb into the passenger seat. I dump all the bags in the footwell and sit back. I assume he knows where he's going, but ask anyway, "Where are we going?"

"Prestbury," he replies.

"Mm-hmm," I murmur. Checks out so far.

I stare out of the window and then hear a static noise. I look over to see it's coming from a small radio in the middle of the dash.

I bite the inside of my lip when I realize that we are hooked up to the police radio and that they are talking about a huge explosion on the outskirts of the city. Aidan turns it up. That's all the confirmation I needed that Ruby set off the explosion.

I gulp.

I know she isn't a terrorist. She must've had a good cause to do what she did. She *knows* the shit I've been through with this. It was a while ago, back in 1996. I was only six years old when the Arndale Centre was blown up. My mum and I were walking there from the train station when it went up. I remember the screams, the fear, the smell, the *noise*. It still gives me nightmares. I shudder, going cold. No, Ruby wouldn't have done that if there were people inside. I know she isn't cold-hearted. She has darkness, I know that, and I accept it. Who doesn't have demons that haunt them? But she isn't a cold-blooded killer.

I look back out of the window, trying to block out the radio. I need to get to Ruby and make sure she is okay and hear from her with my own two ears that she did this for a good reason.

Not that it would change anything if she didn't. I love her and nothing will ever change that. I just hope that when she kissed me earlier, she meant it. I press my fingers to my lips and smile. If I didn't know better, I'd say that there was a slice of jealousy in her eyes when she asked about the 'fluffy-slipper wearing skank.'

I am so glad that my plan worked, but this is only the beginning. I have loved her for a long time, but she has only just seen me for who I really am. There is no way I'm that lucky she will fall in love with me instantly. It's going to take time and I have to show her that she can love me, and count on me. Harassing her about this explosion is something that will have to wait. I hope that she brings it up first, but if she doesn't, then I'll drop it for now. I cannot jeopardize the shaky ground we are on right now. Not for anything. Not even this.

Chapter Twenty-Seven

Ruby

My initial thought is that something has happened to one of my family. My blood runs cold as I hobble to my dad, leaning casually against the black car, his dark sunglasses on, even though it is still raining.

"*That's* her dad?" I hear Ramsey mutter, but ignore him.

"Is everyone okay?" I ask before I reach him.

"Fine," he says and stands up straight.

He is a man of few words. I get that, but jeez. Sometimes he makes me want to scream.

"What are you doing here?" I ask, slipping into his arms for a reassuring hug that was desperately needed after this hellish day.

"Go inside," he says and turns to give Ramsey and Layton a thorough glaring at before he offers to help the injured Ramsey inside my house. I open up and enter the sitting room, watching as my dad helps Ramsey inside and then Layton follows with Declan closing the door behind us.

Ramsey slumps into an armchair and I go to him, running my hand over his head. "I'm sorry," I mutter.

He shakes his head. "This wasn't your fault." He grabs my hand and kisses it, doing a good job of ignoring my dad's eyes on him.

"We need to stitch that up," Declan says quietly and disappears into the kitchen. I wonder how he knows where the first aid kit is. But then figure, seeing as he managed to get in here like a ninja while I was sleeping, it probably isn't the first time. He's probably had a good poke around. With a smile I can't help, I wonder what he thought about the box under my bed.

"So?" I direct this at my dad, folding my arms across my chest in an effort to appear stronger than I feel right now. I need to lie down and sleep for a week, but that's not going to happen anytime soon.

"I came to check on you," he states, standing on the other side of the couch where I fucked Layton.

That inappropriate thought enters my head and now, it's all I can think about. I avert my eyes and clear my throat.

"Uhm," I stammer and then pull myself together. "Why?"

"Because you are my daughter and you are in deep shit," he replies.

"Gee, thanks," I mutter. "I can handle myself."

"I know you can, I made sure you could, but Ruby..." he sighs and removes his sunglasses. "This life...it's not what we wanted for you."

"You don't get a say," I snap. "Not when you are keeping secrets."

"What secrets?" he asks, dark eyes narrowed.

"How do you know Declan?" I ask. This is so not how I wanted to do this. I hadn't even processed it yet. I don't even know *what* there is to process. It's a shitshow.

He grimaces at me. I think he is going to deflect when he opens his mouth to speak, but instead, he says, "I know

Declan from a long time ago. We both used to work for your Great Uncle Teddy."

"As a what?" I ask sarcastically. "An assassin?"

"Yes," he replies steadily and the blood drains from my face. "I used to be a contract killer."

* * *

My eyes fly open, which confuses me. One minute I was standing listening to my dad tell me he was a killer for hire and now I'm lying on the sofa with four men hovering over me.

"I'm fine," I grit out and shoo them away as I sit up. Great. I passed out. What a way to be strong.

I glare at my dad and then at Declan. He knew all of this and didn't tell me. Asshole.

He holds his hands up and shakes his head. "Not for me to say, Princess." Then his cheeks go an adorable shade of red as he fries under the simmering gaze of Rex – the contract killer.

Fuck's sake.

What is this?

"Does Mom know?" I ask quietly.

"Cassie knows about me," Dad replies. "She doesn't know about you."

"Good," I say, breathing out in relief. "Let's keep it that way." It's not that I'm ashamed, but she won't understand. Or maybe she would if she knows about her husband's past. Past? Or present?

"Do you still do that work?" I croak out.

He shakes his head.

I know I shouldn't be so prudish about this given what I do, but it really icks me out to know that my own father is a killer. One like Declan. Cold and frightening.

I push my hair out of my face and sigh. Luckily, we are all saved from further awkwardness when the door opens and

David strolls in, bringing with him his cheerful mood. I smile up at him gratefully as he drops the bags he's carrying on the floor and takes us all in, his hazel eyes landing on my dad with curiosity.

"David, this is my dad," I murmur.

"Oh," he says and holds his hand out. "David Jones. Ruby's assistant."

Dad glares at David's extended hand and for a moment, I think he is going to be rude and ignore it, but he takes it and shakes it firmly. "Rex," he mutters.

David nods and raises an eyebrow at me. I shrug. Rex is Rex.

I make a motion to stand up and then hiss. I look down at my leg to see that while I was unconscious, nimble fingers sliced the leg of my leather pants wide open and used the steri-strips in the first aid kit to close up the bullet graze on my thigh.

"Nice work," I mutter and stand up, favoring my injured leg. "I need a shower and then we can talk. I can't think right now," I add to my dad.

"Sure," he says and sits down, making himself comfy in the chair by the fire.

"David, would you mind helping me?" I ask.

"Of course," he says and ignores dad's hard gaze.

He's doing a lot of that at the moment. He's not stupid. He knows something is going on somewhere. I just hope he doesn't decide to make an issue out of it today. I'm not in the mood.

I give Ramsey a soft smile and he gives me a tired one back. I need some time alone with him, but he can't help me right now. I lead David down the hallway to my bedroom and close the door behind us. I don't say a word as I go into the bathroom.

He follows me. "What do you need me for?" he asks.

"Help me out of these pants," I say, trying not to make it sassy or seductive. I literally just need someone to help me take these shredded leather pants off without hurting my leg. Now that the adrenaline has faded, I'm aching, and the wound is burning like the fires of hell.

"Oh yeah?" he asks, taking it as I didn't mean it, but I'm quite glad he did.

"I'm sore," I whine, and he chuckles.

"I can see that, but didn't think you'd ever mention it."

"I know when to ask for help," I retort. "As in now?" I gesture to my pants.

His gaze heats up and it makes him unbelievably attractive. That look of desire on his face aimed at me makes my heart beat faster. Where has all of this come from?

My breath hitches when he moves in closer. He reaches out to undo the buttons on my leather waistcoat first. After he takes that off, he silently lifts up the hem of my long-sleeved tee and slowly pulls it up over my head.

His eyes drop to my breasts, encased in a sexy lace bra. "Beautiful," he murmurs, making me shiver.

His fingers skate lightly over the fabric until he unclasps it at the back, letting it drop and watching as my breasts tumble free. My nipples peak enticingly.

He licks his lips but doesn't touch. He slowly trails his hands down my stomach to the top of my pants. He flicks the button open and lowers the zipper, then he drops to his knees and pulls my pants down, careful not to touch the bandaged wound on my leg.

Placing my hand on his shoulder for support, I step out of them. I'm in front of him in just my black lace thong, but to my delight that doesn't last very long. He stands up quickly and grabs my hips, lifting me up onto the counter.

He hooks his fingers into the sides of the panties and pulls down. I lift my ass up so he can remove them from me and drop them on top of the rest of my clothes. He bends down and cups my face, pressing his lips to mine in a soft kiss that makes me moan and open up. He sweeps his tongue over mine. I let him take control of the kiss. As much as I want to dominate him, I just can't right now.

He is an excellent kisser. Not that I doubted it. I hadn't even thought about it until this moment.

"I want you," he murmurs against my lips. "Can I have you?"

"Yes," I whisper back. "Right here."

He groans softly and kisses me again, sweeping my loose hair off my neck to bunch up tightly in his fist.

My clit twitches in response to that, but I won't make any demands from him. Not today. He releases me to unzip his pants. I reach inside to pull out his cock, licking my lips when I find him already hard and ready for me. I stroke him, enjoying the silky smoothness of his long length.

"Do we need to talk about protection?" he rasps.

"Not unless you want to," I reply with a smile.

He laughs nervously back. "Not really," he says and grabs my ass, pulling me closer to him.

I tilt my hips, wrapping my legs around him, ignoring the shooting pain that fires through my injured thigh.

He drops his lips to mine again and lets me guide his cock into my wet pussy. I don't need warming up. I'm so turned on by this slow, careful seduction, I just want to ride him until he bursts.

He thrusts his hips forward, entering me quickly, a groan escaping his lips. I grab his head and kiss him again, shoving my tongue into his mouth in a rhythm that matches his thrusting. I start to pant, feeling the tension of the day start to drift away.

I hear a noise at the door and turn my head sharply, but see only Layton standing there, a heated look in his eyes.

"Thought you might need help," he murmurs.

"Nope," David pants, thrusting wildly. "Don't need any help."

I giggle.

"No, doesn't look like you do," Layton says with a smirk at me.

"Can he join in?" I murmur to David. "Hands only?"

"Be my guest," David rasps. "But he's not having you until I'm finished...can't stop...fuck...Ruby..."

Layton approaches us like a predator. I throw my head back, pushing my tits out for him to twist roughly, I gasp, my clit pulsating madly at the harsh touch.

He wastes no time in dropping his hand to my pussy. His fingers glide over my slippery clit, rotating slowly at first and then speeding up. I thank my lucky stars that David doesn't give a flying fuck that another man is touching me, helping to bring me to an orgasm that I know is going make my whole body shake with unfettered arousal.

"Fuck, yes!" I cry out as the climax hits me hard and fast.

My pussy clenches around David's cock, which makes him groan and thrust deeper until he unloads inside me, coming long and hard with a feral noise that excites me.

Layton's soft pants brush my sweaty hair from my forehead as he leans in closer, then he slips his fingers inside me, while David's dick still fills me up.

"Jesus!" I scream as the action makes me tremble again in their arms. "Yes! Yes!"

Chapter Twenty-Eight

Ruby

Layton lets out a low growl as I clench around his fingers. I want to rip at his clothes, but seriously, I need to get in the shower and go back and see my dad or he is going to wonder what the fuck happened to me and come and investigate. I pull his head down for a rough kiss, He removes his hand from inside my pussy and chokes me slightly before he releases me, and I turn to David.

He grins at me. "Well, that's something we haven't done before," he jokes.

"Yet, we will do it again," I retort and unwrap my legs, slipping his dick out of me. "Um, I suppose it's a bit late in the day to be telling you this, but the other men, Ramsey, Layton and Declan..."

"Yes, yes," he says, waving it off and doing up his pants. "I am under no assumptions that we are exclusive. Well, *I* am," he adds with a frown. "You know that, right?"

I giggle. "You do you," I murmur, knowing he has other needs.

"No," he says, shaking his head. "Ruby. If you want me in whatever capacity, that is it for me. I need you to understand that."

I bite the inside of my lip, taking him seriously, but now isn't the time to bring up what he plans to do when he wants some male-on-male time, with Layton standing here listening with interest.

It occurs to me that I should make some changes over there as well. "Layton," I say, drawing his eyes to mine. "If you are amenable, I would like to further our relationship into something more meaningful than sex."

He snorts in my face, shaking his head in disbelief. "Sure," he says. "I am here to service you in whatever way you see fit."

"What does *that* mean?" I choke back my indignation.

"Exactly that. Like David over here, I'm not interested in being with anyone else. We have been together *once*, and it fulfilled me more than several months of a regular relationship with another woman. You are it for me, Ruby. You bring me a peace that I never knew existed and I cannot lose you. You are free to do whatever you want, with whoever you want, but I'm not going anywhere."

His intense gaze makes me squirm slightly. I gulp and take in precisely what has happened in the last few minutes. I wasn't looking for lifelong declarations, but it does please me that they are both not going to engage with anyone else. Makes things less complicated.

"I need to shower," I murmur. "Help me?"

"I got this," Layton says and turns to the shower to turn it on. Once the water is at a suitable temperature to my carer, he picks me up and places me gently in the cubicle, making sure my leg is sticking out and not getting soaking wet. He picks up the sponge and soap and starts to clean me off while David watches intently. Then he starts on my hair, and I close my eyes, enjoying this immensely. He sure can stick around. I want this on a regular basis.

"You are so good at this," I murmur as he towels me dry a few moments later.

"I told you I know how to take care of my woman. And you are *my* woman, Ruby."

"I know," I whisper. "And you are mine. You all are."

He grins up at me from the floor, where he is on his knees, drying my feet.

Fuck, but it's the sexiest thing I have ever seen. This dangerous, alpha male, mountain of a man, on his knees in front of me, taking care of me.

Who knew I would want this so badly, I'm aching for it?

He sits me down as David picks out my clothes and then he dresses me. I do absolutely nothing to help him and he revels in it, being so gentle and careful of my injury.

When I'm dressed and David has given my hair a really quick blow out, I'm ready to face my dad again. I stand up and with a smile of thanks at the two men, I head back out into the lion's den.

"About time," he grouses, standing up impatiently.

I ignore him and go to Ramsey. He looks thoroughly exhausted, but Layton has done a good job of patching him up. I tilt his chin up and he smiles at me.

"Do you feel up for a shower?" I ask him.

"Do I look that bad?" he responds.

I giggle. "Kind of," I reply. "But it will ease your aches and pains."

"Yeah," he says and stands up unsteadily.

"Layton," I ask, and he is there, helping Ramsey. "Can you work your magic on him?"

He grimaces at me. "He can shower himself," he growls. "But I'll stay to make sure he doesn't topple over."

139

Ramsey snorts. "Yep, quite able to shower myself, but thanks."

I nod and watch them disappear down the hallway and then turn to David. He waves and follows them, which leaves me, Dad and Declan.

I fold my arms and give my dad a furious glare. "You had no right to have someone follow me around," I snap.

He glowers at me. "I have every right. I am your father and I let you down when you needed me the most. I will *never* allow that to happen again. This..." He comes closer and brushes the back of his hand over my bruised cheek. "...this should never have happened." He gives Declan the most menacing glare he has in his arsenal and if *I* was on the receiving end of it, I'd be shitting myself. Declan, on the other hand, doesn't seem that phased.

"I can take care of myself," I mutter, turning from him. "I've had little time to process what you've told me. I know you did because you know I can handle the truth, yet you treat me with kid gloves. Why?"

"I know how strong you are, Ruby," he says. "But I will never stop looking out for you."

"So why are you here? Really?" I turn back to him, expecting the truth.

I get it.

And I kinda wish I hadn't asked.

"One last job," he says defiantly. "I am here to take out Jake Noonen and keep you safe."

Chapter
Twenty-Nine

Declan

I knew this was coming, but I still freeze as the silence goes chilly. Only Ruby can give me the chills like that. It's strange. No one fazes me. Not a single living person, not even Rex. But his daughter? Yeah, she is something else altogether.

"Like hell you are!" she spits out a few seconds later.

"Ruby," Rex says exasperated. "You are my daughter, and you need to be kept safe. What if that had been you and not your man?"

She blinks.

Her only reaction to Ramsey being called *her man*. I wish Rex knew that I was also her man. Well, actually, I suppose he does now. My slip up in calling her *Princess* before, definitely did not go unnoticed by him. Nothing gets past him. He probably already deduced that everyone here is involved with her in some capacity. It doesn't take a genius to figure out that something happened with her and David when they disappeared.

"Jake wouldn't dare," she hisses. "He is a coward. He has sent someone else after me and then went after the person he thinks I care about most here because of one eavesdropped conversation."

"He plays by a different set of rules than you," Rex hisses back.

"I know that!" she snaps. "He works in *my* town. He is a low-life mob wannabe, running drugs and prostitution rings. He has no real power, only muscle. *I* have the power here and he is making a play for it. There is no way in hell, I'm giving that up to the likes of him. Or Scott," she adds with a growl.

I want to go to her and calm her down. She is getting way too worked up and it's not good for her stress level. As hard as she is, as strong as she is, her mental state is delicate. If she doesn't have an outlet for all that rage, it will crush her. The 'Daddy' in me is aching to help her, but right now is not that time.

"It makes no difference. He is a threat to you," I say, and then wish I hadn't backed up her father. What was I thinking? Even though I mean it, I should've kept my mouth shut.

She turns on me with a furious face. "*I* am a threat to him, and it's about time he remembered that," she says, jabbing herself in the chest.

"And we come full circle to me taking him out. End of story," Rex says, folding his arms over his chest.

"No!" she spits out. "If anyone takes him out, it's going to be me."

"I agree," I say quietly, risking the wrath of Rex but it's a fact.

She opens her mouth to blast me, until she realizes I have her back this time. She shuts it again, her eyes conveying her pleasure at my support. Not that it will make much difference with Rex. He is fuming, with both me and her.

"Not a chance. You are not a killer," Rex snarls.

"No?" she asks coldly. "Tell that to you know who."

Rex flinches visibly at that.

It's all I can do not to go to her. I clench my fists so I don't. It's the last thing she needs right now.

"That was different," he grits out.

"Whatever," she mutters. "But let me explain to you how this works."

I snort at her patronizing tone. Rex's face is one of utter dumbfoundedness. It's pretty hilarious.

She glares at me, and I press my lips together.

Turning back to her dad, she says, "Look, Dad. I get that you want to protect me. I do. But that's not how this works. For starters, if Jake was taken out, it just leaves a hole for someone to fill. That means street gang wars flooding my city and I won't allow that. For all the power I have in the underworld, I don't have the power to shut his operation down. It's too big, there is too much demand. I have no desire to get involved in that unless I absolutely have to. Secondly, how would it look if Jake was killed, and anyone found out it was my *dad* who did it and not me? I would never recover from that. The power of the underworld is so fragile, so delicate, all it takes is *one* domino to fall and the whole castle comes crashing down. This may not be the life you all wanted for me, but it's *mine*. I have worked way too hard and for way too long to lose it and I'm definitely not letting it go for the sake of some vendetta. I will deal with Jake in my own time, in my own way. He is an arrogant son of a bitch who thinks he has power. He doesn't. Not compared to me. You will not lift a finger to help me out of this situation, do I make myself clear?"

My heart pounds in my chest. I am so turned on by her right now, I want to break all of our rules and whisk her to her bedroom to fuck her senseless. I have never loved a woman before. Sure, I've come close. Maybe even thought once or twice that I was, but when I look at her, facing off with her father, defending her power, her city, I know that all of those previous relationships meant nothing. She touches the darkness inside me that needs feeding, but she brings a shred of light with it that I sorely need, or risk being lost in the job. I don't want that. Not again. Once was enough, and the day that Rex rang me up to ask me to watch over her was the day that I was pulled out of that pit. I don't ever want to go back because that means losing her. She is a dark angel, and she revels in the murk, but she still has her humanity. She still has light in her that she enjoys and needs to survive. I *need* that for her because I love her so completely, it will destroy me if she falls too far into the pit.

"And while we are having an honest conversation for once," she continues. "How dare you set your lapdog on me." She gestures wildly to me.

The insult hits me hard. "Hey," I croak out.

"I don't need watching," she says, ignoring me.

"Yes, you do. I hear you about Jake and I respect your decision to take care of this yourself, as much as I hate it and as much as I am going to worry about you until I go gray. But Declan is non-negotiable. He has been protecting you for years, and you have needed it, Ruby, even if you don't think so."

I gulp. Aw shit.

"Years?" she asks incredulously and turns to me. "You said you'd been here six months."

I exchange a glance with Rex. He raises his eyebrow at me, but I look away and force myself to meet her furious green eyes again. "I have been," I say carefully. "The man who was looking out for you was hired by me when I had other jobs to do. He was one of the best men I knew, but he was killed in action and that's when I knew I had to give up the rest of my work and focus solely on you."

"You mean my dad made you," she spits out.

"No," I say calmly. "It was my decision."

"Ugh," she mutters. "You two are as bad as each other. I am old enough to make my own decisions and to take care of myself."

"Declan is not going anywhere," Rex says.

"He works for me now, by the way," she says. "Did he not tell you that?"

"No," Rex growls menacingly. "He did not."

Ah feck. Busted.

I shrug.

It wasn't devious on my part. I wasn't trying to get double pay; I just hadn't had the time really to fill him in on the change of employment.

"Well," Ruby says with a smug smile at me. "I will leave you two to discuss that." She stalks off, scooping up her phone as she goes, dialing it and saying a moment later, "Beth. Everything okay?" before she disappears down the hallway.

Because I was too busy watching Ruby leave, I'm caught unawares when Rex takes two giant strides in my direction, grabbing my shirt and slamming me up against the wall behind me. His fist connects with my face in the next breath, smashing my cheek and snapping my head back.

"You slimy fucker," he growls. "I should fucking kill you."

"Do that and she will never forgive you," I snap, shoving him away from me.

"You touched her," he snarls. "I hired you to look out for her and you took advantage of her, you piece of shit."

I expect it this time and allow him to get one more shot in. I deserve it.

I grunt as my cheek explodes with pain. "It's not like that," I mutter, clenching my fist, ready to defend myself if he comes at me again.

"It sounds exactly like that," he grits out. "Does she know who you are? What you've done?"

"She knows some of it. She knew my name. It's not surprising that she could figure it out," I reply.

"So she doesn't know it all," Rex scoffs. "That is a house of cards that is going to come crashing down, Declan. If Ruby gets swept up in the crosshairs of that..."

"She won't," I say quickly. "I will make sure of it. I can promise you that I will keep her safe. That was always my mission and now it is something more. I don't want money for this. I'm in love with her."

"Fuck you," he says with disdain. "You are not good enough for her. Don't ever forget who dragged you out of that shithole in Finglas and gave you this life. You were nothing but a low-life scumbag until you met me, so don't pretend that my daughter is in your league. She is way out of it, asshole. You will end, whatever it is that you think you have with her, or I swear to God, despite what she thinks about it, I will fucking kill you."

I take the hits he fired at me. It's all true. I owe him everything. He was my mentor, even though Teddy is the one who recruited me officially, it was Rex who gave me this life. I would probably be dead already if it wasn't for him. But there is no way on God's green Earth I am giving up Ruby just because he demands it.

I glare at him, and he knows. He knows that I won't go down without a fight. It's just a case now of who gets to tell her about my past first. Him or me?

Chapter Thirty

Ramsey

My ribs hurt like fuck, but I force myself to dry off after the most painful shower in history. But however agonizing it was, there was no way I was asking Layton, or David to help me. I stare at myself in the mirror above the basin in Ruby's fancy bathroom and wince. I look a right sight. I lift my hand up that Layton bandaged carefully to see blood seeping through where my nails should be. I had to get it wet, there was no choice about that. I wrap the towel around my waist and delicately prod my ribs. Not broken, but really sore.

I sigh and head back into Ruby's room where Layton and David are waiting. "Is she okay?" I ask.

"She's fine," David replies. "Don't worry about her. She will only get mad that you're fussing. Are *you* okay?"

"Yep, right as the Manchester rain."

"Of which there is plenty," David says and with a nod, he adds, "I will leave you to it. I had better get back to Black Widows before it gets busy."

I wave him off and give Layton a speculative look. "Is she really okay?"

"Yes," he replies. "She is tough."

"Yeah, maybe too much."

"Don't blame yourself for this. She knows it has nothing to do with you."

"I know, but still. She got hurt because, like an idiot, she came in to save me. Where were you? Or Declan?"

"At her back," he replies steadily.

He is being a bit off. I feel there is something he wants to say.

"What is it?" I ask, crawling into bed and hoping Ruby doesn't mind if I lie down for a little bit.

"What's what?" he asks evasively.

"You have something to say about her. I've known you for a long time, Lay. Out with it."

He heaves a sigh and finally looks me in the eye. "She wants more from me. And she is also now involved with David."

"Yeah, I figured about David. He looked like the cat that got the cream," I snort.

"Are you pissed off?"

"Nope. It's up to Ruby who she wants to be with. If that's just me, fine. If it's all four of the men that are currently hovering around her all the time, then that's also fine. *She* is the one with all the power and I'm happy with that. Don't feel like you have to skirt around the issue, Lay."

The look of relief that crosses his face tells me all I need to know. He is falling in love with her. I get it. I've worked for her for several years and each passing day was just another day for me to fall for her. It would be selfish of me to want to keep her all to myself.

"Did she fuck David earlier?" I ask the burning question.

"Yeah," Layton replies with a smirk. "In the bathroom."

I chuckle. "Guess that leaves me." I'm not bitter about it, even though I'm the one that's supposed to be romantically involved with her. We will get there in our own time. I'm not going to rush her. There's no need or no point in that. I get the feeling that she has been badly burned in that area. What she wants from me is different from what I expected. I thought she would be all dark all the time with sex, but that's not what she said. She wants 'normal' with me. I'm cool with that. Layton said that the other women I've been with are vanilla and it's true. Beautiful, wealthy, sexy, vain creatures that balk at the mention of anal never mind a bit of knife play. I have these urges that I want to let loose on Ruby, so I hope she will bend in that area for me.

"Not so sure Declan has been with her in that way," Layton mutters, interrupting my thoughts.

"Hm. There's definitely something going on with them though."

"Yes, it runs deep and dark," Layton says, looking me dead in the eye. "It is something that no one can compete with."

I nod, taking in the warning. Not that I would interfere. Declan is...I wouldn't say scary, but he is not someone I would cross easily. I respect that. Hopefully he respects what I have growing with Ruby as well. He saw us together and heard our conversation earlier and didn't make a fuss, so I'm going to assume he won't make waves.

"You look knackered," Layton says. "Get some sleep."

I nod, suddenly exhausted now that sleep has been mentioned. I think my usual couple of hours will see dust as soon as I close my eyes.

I really need to speak to Ruby, but it will have to wait now. She has other shit going on with her dad here and whatnot. My head hits the pillow and my eyes close of their own accord. I hear Layton open the door and a muttered conversation between him and Ruby before she comes in and heads straight

149

for the bed. She climbs in and strokes my face. I smile and grab her hand, kissing it.

"Sleep," she murmurs.

"Will you hold me?"

She hesitates. That screams that she doesn't like that kind of intimacy in bed. I'm about to let her off the hook when she snuggles down and places her head on my chest. Luckily my bruised ribs are on the other side, so I hold her gently and fall asleep with the woman I love in my arms.

Chapter Thirty-One

Ruby

A soft grunt wakes me from a dead sleep. I crack an eye open to see that the day is growing dark. That means I've been asleep for about three hours or so. My tongue is glued to the roof of my mouth and my eyelids feel like lead, but I sit up, on alert at the noise.

"Get back in bed," I chide Ramsey, who I have caught sneaking out.

He chuckles. "You coming on to me?"

"Don't think you're up for a round of hide the sausage," I snort. I love this about him. I can be light and free with him and it's...easy.

He lets out a loud laugh and shakes his head. "You'd be right. But I need to get going. Work."

I frown. "What?" I snap. "You can't go to work."

"Look, Ruby. I know you have this thing with relationships with employees, but it's tough shit. I'm not quitting. I need to know that you're safe and if working on the door at

Widows is the only way to do that, then that's what I'm going to do, and you will have to accept it."

"Oh, I don't expect you to quit. The whole working for me ship has sailed and is halfway to New York by now. But..." I reach over the nightstand and pick up my phone. I chuck it at him. He extends his arm to catch it and then grunts clutching at his side. "...see where I'm coming from?"

He throws my phone on the bed with a scowl. "I'm working and that's final."

"As your boss, I'm telling you no."

"As your boyfriend, I'm telling you, you don't get a say," he retorts.

And this is why I never wanted to mix business with pleasure. I sigh and fold. I hate that I have to fold. I hate folding. I'm not a fucking folder and yet here I am folding like a tent with no poles. "Fine," I mutter. "But if shit kicks off and you can't do your job, I will fire your ass so fast, you won't know what hit you."

"Got it, Boss," he says with a soft smirk. He approaches me and tilts my chin up with his good hand. "Kiss me," he demands.

I part my lips in preparation. He presses his to mine and sweeps his tongue against mine. He is such a good kisser, it makes me want to drag him back into bed and ride him until the cows come home, but that would require his active participation and I really don't think he is up for it. It's disappointing, but I eventually let him go before my arousal shoots off the chart from this one sensual kiss and I abandoned common sense.

"Go," I rasp. "I will see you there in a bit."

He pulls back. "You're coming in?"

"Have to. Haven't been in the casino for a couple of nights. People will notice. I also have to drop in at the other two at some point tonight."

"Get Declan to drive you, yeah?"

"If I must," I say, a bit miffed still about him and dad and their little buddy system. At least Declan had my back about Jake. But then, it is the least he can do after his deviousness.

"See you soon," Ramsey says and ambles off.

I inhale deeply and flop back to the bed, for a moment, wanting to go back to sleep, but I need to get up and do what I said.

I drag my stiff body out of bed and stretch. I shove my phone into the pocket of my sweats that I didn't even bother changing out of when I crawled into bed. I hobble for a few steps, feeling the pain in my leg subside the further I walk.

"Shake it off, Rubes," I mutter to myself.

Walking through the sitting room, I find it empty and head into the kitchen under no assumptions that my dad or Declan have left.

I'm correct. They are both in the kitchen, on opposite sides, my dad hunched in a chair at the small round table in the corner, bruised knuckles on show and Declan is leaning against the counter near the fridge/freezer, a bag of frozen mixed veg held up to his face.

"Oh, for fuck's sake!" I snap at them. "What is this about?"

"Nuthin'" Dad mutters.

"Yeah, right," I growl and turn to Declan, expecting him to answer.

He averts his gaze, which surprises me, and says nothing.

I sigh and ignore the situation because I can't really be bothered to chase up the cause of this fight if neither one is willing to share.

"I'm heading into work," I announce.

Dad stands up quickly, shoving the chair back so hard, it topples over. "Not a chance," he growls.

"Stand down," I say calmly, not rising to this again now

that I've had some sleep and my leg isn't feeling quite so sore. "If I don't, I might as well just hand my business over to Jake or Scott or Maverick, or anyone who wants it." I turn to Declan; his blue eyes are full of something akin to worry but that can't be right. I narrow mine at him. "You coming?"

"Yes," he says instantly.

"Ruby, wait," Dad says. "We need to talk."

"So do we," Declan says hurriedly.

I give them both an annoyed glare. "Dad. No offense, but go home. I love that you came here to try and help, but seriously, there is nothing you can do. Declan, be ready to drive me into the city in about half an hour."

"Ruby," Dad says, a warning in his voice, but I hold my hand up.

"Big girl, Rex," I say, using his name to drive home that I'm an adult now and can take care of myself. "Go back to Mom and tell her I'm okay." I frown. "Actually, what *did* you tell her?"

He grimaces. "I told her I was going on a business trip," he admits sheepishly.

I stifle the urge to berate him. I also suppress the shiver that threatens to creep down my spine. Business trip to kill. I cannot believe my dad has kept this secret all these years. I see why he did, but still, if he knew what I was into, why didn't he tell me sooner? I wish he had.

"Are you going to tell her about me?" I ask quietly.

"Not my secret to tell, Ruby, that's on you."

That's a dad's guilt trip if I ever heard one.

He comes over to give me a hug and whispers in my ear. "You need to speak to Scarlet, ask her about last summer."

I rear back sharply. "What do you mean?"

"Just ask her," he says, and then gives Declan a hard look.

I look between the two men, confusion clouding my

ability to think straight. "Okay," I mutter, wondering what the fuck he is talking about.

"If anything happens to her, I'm holding you personally responsible," Dad snarls at Declan, no love lost there, it seems.

"I will protect her with my life," Declan growls back.

"Ugh," I mutter and exit the kitchen, eager to get away from the testosterone flying around. I pull my phone out of my pocket and call my sister. She lives in Liverpool, so not far from me, but we are both so busy we hardly get to see each other anymore. I get her voicemail. "Scar? Rex said I need to ask you about last summer. Give me a call, sister." I hang up and head back into my bedroom to get dressed in something so sexy, Declan will lose his shit. I have decided that we need to redefine our relationship. I still want him to be my Daddy and I need everything he gives me in that area, but even though there is a lot of crap we need to sort out, there is something so unbelievably attractive about him and his darkness that I want – no *need* – to explore it on a more personal level. I'm drawn to him in ways that make my pussy wet and my heart speed up at the thought. I won't lie that what he does for a living is a big part of that.

Am I fucked up or what?

Chapter
Thirty-Two

Ruby

I sort through my closet to find the right dress to wear. I land on a slinky, red silk number with thin straps, which skims my body perfectly and has a split up my left thigh. Pulling it out, I take it off the hanger and undress quickly including my underwear. I've already selected a red, lacy strapless bra with matching thong, which I throw on quickly. Then I step into the dress and pull it up, sliding up the side zipper. I step into a pair of red heels and then grab the two knives from the nightstand where they were placed during my unconsciousness and fix-up. I grimace as I pull the dress up and attach the right holster much higher than I'm used to so I can avoid the wound and then repeat the process with the left one to avoid the split. I brush out my wavy, black hair and then pick up my phone where I threw it on the bed after calling Scarlet. I glance at the screen. She hasn't called me back yet. It's not surprising. Her job is at odd hours so she could still be sleeping at this time.

I saunter out to the sitting room where I stop, my breath

catching in my throat. "Well, fuck," I breathe out when I spot Declan decked out in a black tux he pulled out of somewhere, staring into the mirror above the sideboard where I keep my handgun, a bow tie loose around his neck.

He meets my eyes in the mirror and smiles. "Could say the same to you," he says and lifts up the end of the bow tie.

"Leave it," I blurt out.

He raises an eyebrow at me and turns around, dropping the bow tie. He undoes the top two buttons on his shirt.

"Yes," I breathe out like a fool. "You are a handsome fucker, aren't you?"

He lets out a soft laugh, the amusement actually reaching his eyes. "Well, I knew you would come out of that bedroom looking like a goddess. I had to measure up."

"And you just walk around with a tux in your back pocket?" I ask, preening at the goddess compliment.

"In the boot of my car. My *real* car, which is now in your driveway," he replies.

"Handy," I murmur.

He approaches me slowly, almost stalking me. "We need to talk," he murmurs, taking a lock of my hair and twirling it around his finger. He appears mesmerized by it momentarily before he meets my eyes.

"Yeah, we do," I reply and draw in a deep breath.

His eyes flicker with worry, but he smiles. "You start?"

I nod. "I know I said we were over, but then we had the time in my office, and it made me realize that I can't lose you. I need what you give me."

He gives me a slightly confused look before his face goes neutral again. "What are you saying?" he murmurs.

"That I want to resume our DD/LG relationship, if you want to," I whisper, suddenly afraid that he is going to reject me.

"I want that," he whispers.

I nod, relieved, but there's more I have to say. I don't know how he will react to it. I take a breath and run my hands up his chest, dropping my phone into the inside pocket of his jacket before I rest them lightly over his pecs. He grabs my fingers. Looking down at them.

"I want more from you," I mutter, grabbing the bull by the horns. I don't know why I'm so nervous saying this to him. With the other men it was easy, I just came out with it and expected them to fall in line. Declan is a whole different ball game. Our dynamic is on a whole different level.

"What do you want, Ruby?" he asks.

"Can we talk in the car?" I ask, chickening out for a minute. I need time to compose myself.

He nods, pulling my hands from his chest and tightening his grip. He restrains my arms at my sides and stares into my eyes. His are full of something I can't figure out and it drives me crazy. I wish I could read him, but I have no idea. Then he drops my hands and grabs my hip with one of his, the other going to the back of my neck. He draws me close and kisses me roughly, his fist tightening painfully in my hair. I meet his aggressive thrusts with my tongue, matching the rhythm he has set. As soon as it gets going, he stops and pulls away, taking my hand and leading me out to the car silently. I lock up and wait for him to open the reappeared Aston Martin. He gallantly opens the passenger door for me to slip inside and I wait, my hands sweating for him to get in. He sets off and after a few minutes, I break the silence.

"How do you feel about expanding our DD/LG relationship to include sex?" I ask hastily.

He glances at me quickly before his eyes go back to the road. He doesn't say anything for a while, clearly contemplating what I said.

"I can't do that," he says eventually, making my cheeks heat up with humiliation at the rejection. "It's not what you're thinking," he says quickly. "I want to have sex with you, Ruby. I have wanted that for a long time, but not in that way. It will tarnish the relationship and I don't want that."

"What do you mean 'tarnish'?" I ask, trying to keep the anger out of my tone.

"It's not what you need from me in that situation. You need to confess your bad deeds, be punished for them and absolved in a way that gives you peace. If we throw sex into that mix, it becomes..." He pauses, searching for the right word. I'm shocked when he finds it and says, "...dirty."

"*Dirty*?" I snap at him, tears pricking my eyes.

"You know I'm right, Princess," he says softly. "That time isn't for sex. Yes, I can cause you pain and then pleasure you, it's part of the process but intercourse isn't right. I don't want that, for you or for me."

I blink back the tears. I think I get what he's saying in a backhanded way.

"You find our time precious?" I ask, hoping I'm right and not about to make a huge fool out of myself.

"Very," he says. "You need it to bring you peace and I need to give that to you. I don't want it sullied by sex."

We pull up at a red light and he shifts the car into neutral and puts the handbrake on. He turns to me, cupping my face again. "That's not rejection, Princess. I want you very much. If you want me in that way, then we have to agree to engage in sex outside of the roleplay. Can you do that, or it is sex with your Daddy that you're looking for?"

My lips part as I search his blue eyes for the answer. "I want sex with you," I whisper. "I don't know how you want to do this?" I lick my lips; my mouth has gone dry.

"Why do I make you nervous?" he asks seriously. "Where is the confident Ruby that grabbed David and kissed him when she had no idea if he would kiss her back?"

"You don't make me nervous," I scoff, but it's a lie. I sigh. "I can't read you," I admit quietly. "It unnerves me."

"I'm an open book for you," he replies.

I blink as a horn blasts behind us and he smiles. "Guess the light is green." He turns back to the road and sets off again.

After a substantial pause, in which I have no idea what to say next, he thankfully breaks the silence. "We will resume our DD/LG relationship in the same way with which we have been, but all the other times, I want a normal relationship with you."

I choke back my laugh. "Normal?" I croak out. "Can you do normal?"

"Can you?" he retorts.

"I can try," I say, "but seriously. What do you constitute as normal?"

He shrugs. "We'll have to see how it goes."

I nod, glad that we have sort of resolved this issue. It's all a learning curve. "The other men?"

"Do what you want with them," he says. "They are no factor for us."

I nod, pressing my lips together.

We drive on in silence, the only sign that he even knows I'm still there is when he grabs my hand and laces our fingers together, until he has to pull it back to drive properly or crash the car.

It's a welcome relief when we finally pull into the parking lot of the bar, which appears to have kicked into club mode slightly early. I guess the explosion outside of the city didn't slow anyone down. I don't wait for him to be chivalrous, I just get out and wait for him to join me. "I'll need to go to Canal Street later on, stop in on the other two."

He nods and takes my hand, leading me to the back entrance.

"Front," I say. "I need to check on Ramsey."

He changes direction, still not uttering a word. He is deep in thought, that much is clear. I hope he isn't going to change his mind about anything we just discussed. It will gut me.

The queue at the front of the bar is long and loud. We skip to the front, and I grin up at Ramsey.

"How's things?" I ask, before he bends down to kiss me. I snake my hand up around the back of his neck, standing on tiptoes, despite my heels. Declan doesn't let my other hand go as I kiss Ramsey in front of everyone. It's the first time that I'm showing the world I have more than one man, and I like it.

"Fine," he says and downs another shot of tequila.

"Ah," I say with a laugh. "Not too much."

"Last one," he says and hands the shot glass back to Benn. I give him a quick smile and then we head through as Ramsey gets lost in the job.

The club is darkened, and the music is thumping loudly.

On impulse, I lead Declan to the middle of the dancefloor and start to move against him. He spins me around so that he is pressed close to my back. His hand slides down my hip, over the silky material of the dress and slips into the split. His fingers crush over the lace of my underwear before he plucks the fabric up and slides his fingers onto my pussy. I gasp at the bold move.

"Have you ever had sex in public before, Princess?" he asks in my ear to be heard over the music.

I shake my head. "I've had sex in public places, but not with people watching."

"Close your eyes," he murmurs, his fingers pressing down on my clit and making me moan softly.

I do as he says, moving to the music as he coaxes my clit into a state of excitement. Suddenly, he thrusts his fingers inside me.

"Imagine everyone is looking at us," he says, finger-fucking me slowly. "Imagine they are watching me fuck you with my fingers and it's turning them on. Can you see it?"

"Yes," I murmur with a shiver.

"Some of the men are touching themselves, wishing you would fuck them," he carries on, sliding his fingers out of my pussy and over my clit, only to thrust back inside. "Will you fuck them, Ruby?"

"No," I pant, starting to sweat.

"Who do you want to fuck in front of all of these people, Ruby?"

"You," I gasp as the beginnings of my climax start to build.

He pulls his fingers out and concentrates solely on my clit until I cry out quietly and come in his arms on the dancefloor of my club.

"Now open your eyes," he says.

I do.

Not a single person is watching us.

They are all too busy with their own lives, their own dancing and drinking.

The disappointment slams into me.

"I can give you that," he purrs in my ear, a smile on his lips. "I know a place."

"So do I," I breathe in slowly to steady the pounding of my heart.

He removes his hand from under my dress and wraps his arms around me. I pull his hand up to my lips and suck them clean of my cum.

He groans and kisses my neck. He bites me softly at first, but then when I squirm against his hard cock, evident through his pants, he bites me harder. He sucks and I know I'm going to end up with a love bite the size of a plum for all to see...

...and I don't care.

Chapter Thirty-Three

Ruby

Grabbing Declan's hand, I lead him from the dancefloor and through to the offices at the back. With a sexy smile, I look over my shoulder to make sure we haven't been followed and then push the button at the end of the corridor to open up the downstairs. We slip through quickly and I close the door behind us. I stand on the platform and look down, seeing it full to capacity. I nod in satisfaction and catch Layton's eyes. He is standing just inside the downstairs door in full work mode. He gives me a nod and then his eyes go back to the floor.

I spot David and lead Declan down the stairs, pulling up next to David, who is a busy bee checking the hidden cameras on his iPad for any cheating or nefarious workings.

"Hey," he says, his eyes lighting up in a way that I have never seen before. "How're you feeling?"

"Better," I say and take a hold of his tie to pull him closer.

He grins and kisses me, cupping my face and delving his

tongue between my lips. "You look ravishing," he murmurs against my mouth.

"Thank you," I say, accepting the compliment in a much humbler way than Declan's. "I'll catch up with you later. I want to speak to Beth."

He nods and I finally, reluctantly, let go of Declan to stride over to Beth.

"Hey, Boss," she says.

"Can we talk?" I ask.

She gives me a curious look, but bobs her head and follows me to the corner of the bar where it is quieter.

"I want you to tell me everything about what happened the other night with Jake," I say.

Her expression goes wary. "It's fine," she says, brushing it off.

"No, it's not. I need to know, Beth."

She huffs out a breath. "He cornered me here at the bar and shoved his hands under my top to grab my tits. That's all."

"Did he threaten you at all?" I ask.

She purses her lips. "He said he would make work shitty for me if I fought him. He grabbed my hair and licked my face." Her revulsion is evident, and I don't blame her. I'd vomit all over my expensive shoes if his tongue came anywhere near me.

"You should have told me all of this before," I say gently.

"I didn't want to cause trouble," she mumbles. "He hasn't been back, so it's all good. Besides, the new guy is shit-hot at stopping any sign of flirtation gone too far. Actually, he is just shit-hot. Where did you find him?" She gives Layton a doe-eyed look that fires up my green-eyed monster.

"It's no trouble," I say, drawing her attention back to me. I have no doubt that Layton has seen how pretty she is. He has eyes, after all, but the thought of them doing anything together makes me feel slightly ill. "I need to know this stuff so I can keep you safe."

She nods. "Honestly, now that he isn't coming around, I'd forgotten about it," she assures me.

I nod and let her go. I don't think she is as fine about it as she is letting on. I call David over.

"Get private security on her, will you? I'm not convinced that Jake is done with her yet."

David nods and pulls out his phone. My eyes wander over to Declan at the bar, taking in his gorgeous self. I just watch him for a few moments, enjoying the sight as David arranges to have Beth watched over twenty-four, seven.

"Done," he says.

I tear my eyes away briefly and nod, looking back at Declan quickly, a frown falling over my face. Something isn't right.

Chapter
Thirty-Four

Declan

I feel Ruby's phone vibrate in my jacket pocket and know instantly it is Scarlet returning her call.

"Dammit," I mutter and pull it out, answering it immediately. "Scarlet."

A pause.

Then she says, "Paddy? What are you doing with Ruby's phone?"

I bite my tongue, wanting to correct her, but that is the name I gave her. An alias of mine that I use now and again. "Scarlet, listen to me. Ruby wants to know what happened last summer. You can't tell her. Please."

"What?" Scarlet says, confused. "What the fuck is going on? Where is Ruby? Let me talk to her."

"Please..." I start.

"Declan?" Ruby's voice sounds out behind me, and I curse silently.

I hang up the phone and slide it back into my jacket pocket. I have no choice now but to tell Ruby everything. I hadn't wanted to ever bring this up. It will hurt her and that is the last thing I want to do. Rex has forced my hand and rather she hears it from me than her sister or her dad.

"Who was that?" she asks, her face a fierce frown.

"No one," I mutter. "Ruby, we need to talk."

"What about?" she asks. I can see the dread in her expression, so I smile and try to relax, but I'm as tense as I've ever been.

I cup her elbow and lead her over to the area under the metal staircase where we can get some kind of privacy. I have to act quickly now. I can see David on his phone, looking at us and making his way over.

"I have something to tell you," I start quickly. "It happened a while ago, before you and I started our role-playing relationship. Please know that it wasn't intentional, and I certainly never thought that we would end up *here*."

"Declan," she says. "You're scaring me."

"I know, I'm sorry. Ruby." I press my hands to my eyes, trying to figure out how to say it. I have seconds before David hands his phone to Ruby and I have no doubt that Scarlet is on the other end, waiting to tell all.

"Declan," Ruby says, icily. "Tell me what's going on."

I inhale sharply. "Last summer..." and I see her face fall. It kills me that she has already deduced what I'm about to tell her. Or at least what she *thinks* happened. "...Your sister and I had a fling, not even...one night," I blurt out right before David reaches us.

Ruby hisses and David freezes, his phone outstretched.

"Hang up," I growl at him.

He does so, but he doesn't leave.

"It's not what you think," I explain hastily, taking Ruby's hands.

She snatches them back and folds her arms, her eyes shooting daggers. But she doesn't say a word.

"I was in a bad place," I mutter. "Really bad. I met her when I was trying to forget my miserable existence, drowning in a bottle of Whisky in a dive bar, when she walked in. She came to me," I make that point very clear. Not that it makes a damn bit of difference. I have minutes, maybe less, before Ruby walks out of here and out of my life, for good. "She started talking to me and I needed someone to talk to. She was there. I have demons, Ruby. Demons that haunt me and she listened. I took her to bed that night, but it was born out of despair. There was no pleasure in it. It was solace. I felt sick to my stomach afterwards and ran out. I haven't seen or spoken to her since. It was *nothing*. It meant absolutely nothing to me. You, Ruby, you mean everything to me. You always have since the day I first laid eyes on you when you were so fragile, so hurt by what happened to you. Please, you have to believe me." I'm rambling desperately. It's what she wants. It's why she hasn't uttered a word yet.

"Did you know she was my sister?" she asks, her tone so dark, it sends a shiver down my spine.

"Yes," I reply. "I knew who she was. I wasn't seeking her out and I haven't sought her out since. It was a mistake that I regret..."

"Save it," she spits out. "Let me fill in the blanks. You started being my *Daddy* right after that, didn't you?"

"Yes," I admit, staring at the floor in shame. "I felt so disgusted with myself, I needed to make it right somehow, even if you didn't know, even if you didn't know *me*."

"So you have fucked *her* and yet you won't fuck me. How do you think that makes me feel?" she asks.

"Ruby," I chide. "You know that's not it. I love you, for fuck's sake. I want to be with you in every single way."

"Love?" she snarls. "You *love* me? You don't even know me. You can't say you love me and then tell her all your secrets and fuck her when it's taken this long for me to find out who you really are."

"I swear, it meant nothing," I beg her. "I barely even remember it. Please, Ruby, I know that it was wrong. I hate myself for it. But I will always tell you everything. Ask me. Ask me anything." I can smell my own fear that she is going to walk out.

It's not unfounded.

She growls at me, slapping my face so hard and then she stalks away, David hot on her heels. She brushes past Layton, who grabs her arm, but she pulls away from him. I storm after her, furious with Rex for this. He wanted this relationship destroyed and he got it. "Ruby, wait! Please!" I call after her.

"Fuck you," she screams at me, marching out into the open air of the dingy alley at the back of the club. It's still fucking raining and mingles with her tears. Her tears that I caused. It stabs me in the heart.

"Ruby, please, listen to me."

"No, I'm done listening to you. I don't want to hear anything else that comes out of your mouth! I'm clearly not the sister you want to be with but the one you got lumbered with!" Her fury is covering up her pain and I wish I could take it away, but I'm the one causing it. I'm floundering. For the first time in my entire life, I have no control over this situation and no idea what to do next.

"Fuck, Ruby, please," I implore her. "I love you, Princess. Please don't turn away from me."

"You need to leave her alone," Layton says, shoving me away from her, having been brought up to speed by David. "Go now."

"No!" I roar, my anger driving my absolute terror that I'm going to lose the only reason I have to draw my next breath. "Ruby!"

"Don't," David says quietly. "Just leave it for now."

169

"I can't," I snap, turning to him. I shove past Layton and drop to my knees in the disgusting, dank alley, dropping into a murky puddle at her feet. I place my hands on her hips and look up at her, the rain dropping onto my face. She glares down at me, those green eyes full of hurt and anger.

"What can I do to prove to you that I love you?" I ask her. "I will tell you anything you want to know. I will do anything you want me to do...just please tell me how to fix this."

She shakes her head, her jaw tight. "You can't fix it, Declan. All I see when I look at you now, is you shoving your cock into my fucking sister. How could you?"

I want to tell her that we weren't together when I did this horrible thing but that will only aggravate her further. She has every right to be hurt.

"There has to be a way. Action over words. Just tell me what I can do."

She glares down at me silently, her face rigid and her body stiff.

We are both drenched when she finally opens her mouth to speak. "I don't know, Declan. I honestly don't think there is anything you can do to fix this." She stumbles back and allows Layton to sweep her into his arms, carrying her back inside. David hesitates, placing a hand on my shoulder, but then he too follows, leaving me on my knees, soaking wet, full of self-loathing and scared stiff that Ruby will never forgive me and let me make it up to her.

Chapter Thirty-Five

Ruby

Sitting at my desk, I twirl the knife in my hand. It's the pretty Pangolin Ramsey gave me for my birthday. I run my thumb over the sharp edge and wonder what it would feel like slicing into my skin, making me bleed.

I lift my dress up my thighs, scowling at the bullet graze wound. It's starting to ache again now. Maybe I need to try Ramsey's method of pain killer. Taking a deep breath, I press the edge of the blade to the soft skin of my inner thigh.

"It's not as much fun if you do it yourself," Layton's voice comes through the open doorway quietly.

"Should've shut that," I grit out, but slide the knife back into the holster. That dark shit isn't for anyone else to witness. It's my own secret hell and no one gets to be a part of it. "Who's watching the door?"

"David has me on the walkie if shit kicks off. I need to be up here right now," he replies, sitting down.

"I'm okay," I say. "Honestly. I am. It's my own fault for being fool enough to think he was mine."

"He is yours," he replies, surprising me.

"Oh?" I ask with a raised eyebrow.

"I'm playing Devil's advocate," he says with that sexy smirk. "He is currently drowning his sorrows downstairs and is about to do something really fucking stupid. Yes, what he did was bad, but you didn't even know him then. Why does it hurt so much?"

"Because he told her things about himself. I know fuck all. Fuck. All." I get angry all over again. It isn't even about the sex. So, he has a past. So do I. So does Scarlet. Who gives a shit who banged who way back when? It's the fact that she *knows* him, and I don't."

"Why haven't you asked him?" Layton's reasonable question pisses me off.

"Haven't had time," I snap.

"And that's his fault?"

"Why are you siding with him? You're supposed to have *my* back."

"I do have your back. I'm trying to fix this because whatever it is he gives you, you need. Is it worth losing him over this?"

"I don't need him," I say petulantly, but we both know it's a lie.

I heave an annoyed breath and ask, "What's he about to do?"

"He is talking about bringing you Jake's head on a platter. Seeing as he is who he is, I'm taking that he means it literally. Now, ordinarily I probably wouldn't interfere, but he is three sheets to the wind on Irish Whisky and he'll fuck it up. Go and talk to him."

"And say what?" I ask with a huff.

"Whatever it is you're feeling."

"Why are you so rational?"

"It's part of my charm," he drawls.

"Ugh!" I exclaim. "Send him up. I don't need a big, fat mess to clean up even if it does mean Jake ends up at the bottom of the ship canal."

"Yes, Ma'am," he chuckles and stands up.

I give him a sly look then. "Seems you have an admirer," I say, almost with a tinge of accusation.

His eyes narrow and he leans down, placing his massive hands on the desk between us. "What are you insinuating?"

I shiver at the menace emanating from him. It's turning me on in all sorts of fucked up ways.

I meet his eyes dead on. "That you'd better behave, or it'll be *your* head on a platter," I say, slowly standing up.

He reaches over the desk and clamps his hand around my neck. "I told you before, sweetheart, that you are it for me. Don't go looking for shit that isn't there. Do I make myself clear?" He squeezes, making me gag slightly. My hands automatically go up to him, but my eyes are blazing with heat.

"You are mine," I choke out. "Don't ever forget it."

"Oh, I won't," he says quietly. "You don't have to worry about me."

"Good," I rasp.

He lets me go and turns to exit my office, leaving me panting and aroused beyond belief, but dissatisfied that I didn't get to finish what I'd started. I wonder if having Layton use my body like a gory sketch pad might do the trick. It's worth a shot because this will niggle at me now until the need to hurt is sated.

I sit back down and wait, drumming my fingers on the table.

Moments later, Declan appears, not quite as drunk as Layton made out. Maybe he has excellent control, or perhaps he can just hide it better than most.

EVE NEWTON

"Ruby," he rasps, his voice hoarse. "I'm sorry..."

"Forget it," I clip out. "I was being overly dramatic earlier."

Wariness fills his eyes as he gives me a cautious look. It's almost as if he is waiting for me to say I'm joking and that he is dead to me.

"I want you to know that I don't care about that sex. Not really," I say carefully. "I didn't know you. I definitely had no claim on you. You were free to do whatever you wanted with whomever. It's the fact that she knows you better than I do that has shat on my parade, but Layton has made me see that it's not the end of the world and all I have to do is ask."

"I will tell you anything you want to know," he murmurs.

"We'll get to that," I say briskly. "Right now, I just want to continue with my night the way it was set out. I need you to sober up so you can drive me to Canal Street later and then drive me home afterwards, where I will expect more groveling in the form of some kind of gratuitous sexual act that satisfies my darkest desires. Can you do that for me, or is it asking too much?"

"Consider it done," he says instantly. He waits a beat and then comes around to my side of the desk to take my hands. "I don't deserve you," he murmurs.

"Yeah, well. We've all got demons, Declan. Mine are big, scary ass motherfuckers and we take comfort where we can, when we can. But let me make one thing very clear to you right now...if you *ever* go to *her* again seeking that comfort, I will fucking slice your throat open, reach in and pull your tongue out of the opening. Is that something you understand?"

"Completely," he says seriously. "But you never have to worry about that. You are the only one I need to give me peace, Ruby. I look at you and my soul feels settled in a way

174

that a million conversations with a million different people won't provide. Is that something *you* understand?"

His penetrating stare touches a part of me, I never even knew existed anymore. It was squashed so long ago by an act that ripped away any sense of peace I had inside me.

"Yeah," I mutter. "I understand."

Chapter
Thirty-Six

Ruby

Much, much later, after Declan sobered himself up with hot coffee and ice-cold water, and after we hit up my other two illegal gambling sites, we pull into my driveway back at home. Once we've entered the house, Declan hands me my phone out of his jacket pocket.

"You'd better ring her back," he says and walks off to the kitchen to give me some privacy.

I grimace at the phone. Twenty missed calls and fuck knows how many texts. Unlocking it, I dial, and she answers on the first ring.

"Ruby?"

"Yeah, it's me, this time," I say with a sigh.

"What the hell is going on? How do you know Paddy?"

Paddy?

I smile to myself that at least he didn't tell her his real name. That kind of makes me feel even better about this whole shitshow.

"He works for me," I mutter, wondering how much he

actually told her. Scarlet knows what I do, but does she know what *he* does? Probably not.

"Humph," she says rudely. "Well, watch your back with that one. He is a fuck boy if I ever met one."

My face falls into a frown. "Oh?" I croak out.

"Yeah, he was quite happy to talk and listen to me and take me back to my place to fuck me senseless, but then gone in the morning before I woke up without a note or another word. Asshole," she grouses.

Fuck her senseless.

I inhale deeply and push it aside. It doesn't matter. It's water under the bridge. "Rex wanted me to know about you two, but I have to wonder why," I say tightly. So far, her story matches up, but I need to hear more.

"Because he's a dick," she spits out. "Maybe he thought he would prey on you or something." She lets out a loud laugh. "In fact, I hope he does so you can...you know..."

I can almost hear the shrug.

One thing is perfectly clear. She does not like Declan, one bit. Or maybe she does, and this is all protesting too much? I already have my dad interfering in this relationship, I don't need my sister doing the same. I really hope she isn't going to be a problem. I have made the decision to forgive Declan for an indiscretion that, quite frankly, isn't even anything to do with me. It's just a damn shame it happened with my sister to his knowledge. I'd hate to have to bring my own sister in line if she starts to meddle where she isn't wanted. A sickening thought suddenly occurs to me, and I have to ask the indelicate question or be bugged about it until the end of time.

"Well, yeah he seems like a bit of a player," I say carefully. "Hope you used protection."

"Please," she scoffs. "What do you take me for? Think I'd touch a one-nighter without him being bagged. Ugh!" Her disgust reassures me that Declan did, in fact, wear a condom and now I don't have to be grossed out by having sex with him without it. I really dislike them immensely. They make me itchy, and I like to feel my man inside me. I take extra precautions for myself with regular testing and birth control, but yeah, it's a matter of trust who I take between my legs. Sadly, it doesn't happen all that often. I have to *really* want it after what happened to me. I like all the play and foreplay and vibrators are a wonderful invention. These four men, though... they have a hold over me that no other man has ever had. They make me *want* them. Scratch that...*need* them. It's a revelation and one I'm looking forward to exploring, despite the fear and uncertainty.

"Rubes?"

Scarlet's voice interrupts my thoughts.

"Yeah."

"You aren't seriously thinking of going there, are you?"

"Nah," I lie. It's just easier that way. "Don't know why Rex wanted me to know all this. It's none of my business."

"Yeah, well," she huffs and then there's an awkward silence.

"It's late, I'd better go and get some sleep," I say.

"Sure," she says. "I'm on a job anyway. This dude is going to kill me for spending so much time away." She laughs and all is well again.

I hang up and check the clock. 3AM. I'm absolutely exhausted but there is no way I'm letting the rest of this night get away from me. David, Layton and Ramsey are meeting us here momentarily and I intend to make the most of it. I dump my phone on the sofa and head into the kitchen.

Declan is leaning casually against the counter, a bottle of water from the fridge in his hand.

"Everything is fine," I say before he can say a word. "She told *you* stuff as well, didn't she?"

He nods carefully.

"I'm not gonna ask, don't get your panties in a bunch," I say wryly. "I just wondered why she was stressing so hard."

"I will tell you if you ask," he says. "I don't want there to be any secrets between us."

"Nope, I don't need to know my sister's business. Whatever she told you, you take to the grave."

He shrugs. "So, are we good, Princess?"

"Yeah," I say with a soft smile, loving that endearment from him suddenly. It makes me feel cherished or some shit. "But I have questions that need answers."

"I know. Shoot," he says, bracing himself for the firing squad.

"What got you into such a state that night that you got drunk and found yourself a plaything for the night? Doesn't seem to be your style and to be honest, I'd think it quite dangerous in your line of work. Loose lips and all that."

His face goes icy before it crumples, and he drops his head into his hands. "It's confession time, isn't it?" he asks rhetorically. "I'll tell you, Princess but you might not like what you hear."

"Try me," I murmur, a shiver going down my spine at his words. He knows me. He knows what I'm capable of. If he thinks I won't like what he has to say, how bad is it?

"It has to do with you and your previous play partner," he starts.

I draw in a sharp breath, taking a defensive step back. "Wh-what about him?" The genuine fear that slices through me takes me by surprise. It sneaks up on me in the darkest hours of the night. Like now. It was bad at the time, but on reflection it was only the paralyzing fear of ghosts from the past that made it so. He stares into my eyes and starts his story, surprising me and kind of turning me on a little bit in the process.

Chapter Thirty-Seven

Declan

"**Y**ou watched me?" she asks, her voice tinged with a deep desire that fires up my engines in a big way.

I was skeptical about admitting to this, but, like I said, no more secrets.

"Yes," I say. "Giselle always sent you to a voyeur's room so I could watch you. It was part of our deal."

"Of which, I need to know more, but later. Go on..."

I take a drink from the bottle of water I'm clutching and continue. "That day, the last time you saw him, I know what he did to you. He abused his power over you. It disgusted me. He degraded you in ways that made me want to kill him. You didn't have to stand for it. You had a safe word, and you didn't use it until it was too late. What he did was rape, and it sickened me..."

I see her about to protest and I hold my hand up to stop her. "I know you don't think so. I know you believe you deserved the punishment he dealt out, but he abused you. Afterwards, when you were crying and cleaning up, he was bragging to anyone who would listen, what he did to you. What he made you do and that he fucked you until you wept and begged him to stop. I knew it was all true and I wanted to go to you, but I was a stranger. You would have run a mile from me and that was something that I couldn't let happen. I went to Giselle and forced her to swap your play partner for me. I needed to know that you were safe in those situations. The only way I could ensure that was for you to be with *me*."

I stop talking, feeling the rage all over again.

"And then what?" she asks carefully, knowing I'm not done yet. Instinctively, she probably knows the worst is yet to come.

"Then I followed that fucker home, took him by the throat and with my bare hands strangled the life out of him. I took great satisfaction in watching the light die in his eyes, knowing that *I* was the one who was giving him his final punishment for treating you so badly."

She lets out a soft gasp, but there is no fear or revulsion in her eyes. If anything, she is turned on. "You killed him? For me?"

"I *murdered* him, and I'd do it again, and again as many times as it takes to keep you safe. I have killed to keep you safe, Ruby and as much as you appear to want to brush that under the carpet, seeing as you have thus far, ignored the fact that my man was killed watching over you, I will lose every bit of what is left of my soul to continue to keep you safe."

"Murdered," she murmurs, making the connection between that and killing.

Killing is my job. It's faceless, nameless, a simple transaction, death in exchange for money. I have no regrets, no guilt over the lives I've taken this way. However, I don't have guilt or regrets for murdering the pervert who abused her body, her mind and her trust. She is everything to me and I will do whatever it takes to make her happy and secure.

She nods, totally getting it and if it was at all possible, I fall even more in love with her. She has no judgement. It's the opposite. It excites her. *I* excite her.

She approaches me stealthily, running her hands up my chest, a look of adoration swimming in her green eyes. She presses her lips softly to mine and murmurs, "Thank you."

I almost weep with the sincerity, the surprise of those two words.

"I have more questions, but they can wait. I want you now. I want you to take me to bed as my lover, before you switch roles and punish me for my part in that."

"No," I croak out, gripping her fingers. "You have *nothing* to be punished for."

"Please," she murmurs, lowering her eyes. "I need it."

"Fuck, Ruby," I whisper, pushing her hair away from her face. "I love you."

She smiles and it's all I can do not to whisk her away to her bedroom and finally fuck her until I want to die in her arms. She needs more. Especially now that those ugly memories have been dredged up. I grasp her arms lightly and turn her, so she is up against the counter. I slide her dress up her thighs, taking the switchblade out of the holster on her right thigh and letting the dress fall back down.

I drop to my knees, hearing her sharp inhalation.

"I hope you aren't too fond of this dress," I say, picking up the hem and flicking the blade out.

She giggles. "Nah, not this old thing."

I give her a slow smile and, keeping my eyes on hers, I slice the fabric of the dress slowly, deliberately upwards, letting it fall apart to expose her perfect body to me. I ignore the scant lace of her thong as I rise to my feet to keep slicing the dress away, all the way to the low neckline. It drops open and I breathe in through my nose as I catch sight of her red lace, strapless bra. I feel her breath on my face as she pants lightly when I lean closer to nick the straps with the sharp blade and the dress drops to the floor at our feet.

I look down and see the slight scratch across her perfect skin and frown, knowing that Layton has had his way with her. But it doesn't matter. All that matters is here and now. I trail the point of the blade down in between her breasts and slice through the lace.

"Now that I did like," she chides me as it falls off her.

"I'll buy you a new one," I murmur and slide the blade down the flawless skin of her stomach where I quickly cut the thin straps holding her knickers together, nicking her skin in the process.

She lets out a feral moan at the slight burn the blade causes, her nipples pebbling, making me want to bite them until she screams.

But I don't. I toss the blade up into the air and watch it flick over. I catch it deftly by the handle and hold it out for her to take.

"Your turn," I say and grin when she takes the knife eagerly, a vicious smile twisting her lips as I give her all the power now.

Chapter Thirty-Eight

Ruby

"Uh," David stammers as he walks into the kitchen to see me naked and brandishing a knife at Declan. "Is this foreplay or should I be worried?"

"Definitely foreplay," I state and flick the knife at the button on Declan's shirt. It pops off and pings on the countertop.

"So all good?" David ventures.

"All good," I confirm. "You see, Declan, here has confessed his sins to me and now he needs to be punished."

"Oh, do I?" he growls at me.

"You do," I say and slice off another button.

"Well, then, Mistress. I am at your mercy."

His devilish smile disarms me. I hadn't expected him to *want* this. I thought he was a Dom through and through. Seems I've got a little Switch on my hands, and they are itching to touch him and make him squirm.

"You like that?" I purr, grabbing his shirt and running the

knife down through the cotton of the remaining buttons so they scatter all at once.

With the blade still in my hand, I shove his jacket and shirt off his shoulders and lick my lips when I see him shirtless and divine. He is spectacularly built. Not bulky muscles like Ramsey and Layton, but slender and tight with abs that make me want to lick them.

I lean down and trail my tongue in between the defined ridges, enjoying his soft moan of pleasure, following up with a rough scrape of the knife.

"Stay," I order David as I sense him about to leave.

"You sure?" he mumbles.

I give him a mock-scathing look. "Obviously. You are as much a part of this as we are."

"You want me to watch?" he asks quietly.

"For now. But I want you to join in later."

"How about we take this to the bedroom, then," he says, coming closer and surprising me when he undoes Declan's belt and starts to lead him out of the kitchen from one end.

Declan takes it all in his stride and follows David, a smirk on his face that makes me smile in delight. I trail after them, wondering if Declan has ever been with a man before. I don't know where the thought came from. Maybe it was seeing him and David in a sexual encounter, as slight as it was. Ramsey and Layton are embroiled in a hushed conversation in the sitting room as I walk in, but they shut up when they see me.

"Care to share?" I ask.

Both sets of eyes laser over me and fill with a desire that makes me feel pretty damn good about myself.

"It can wait," Ramsey says, approaching me quickly, shedding his leather jacket and throwing it on the sofa.

"Okay," I murmur, deciding not to concern myself too much over it. If it was important, I'd like to think they'd come straight out with it.

"So how does this work?" he asks bluntly. "All together or one at a time?"

I burst out laughing because the honesty is adorable and to be fair, I haven't got a fucking clue. I have never had sex with more than one man at a time, ever. The incident in the bathroom with David and Layton was instinct and was hardly a three-way. It was a two-and-a-half-way at best.

"I guess we just play it by ear," I snicker and take his hand to lead him to the bedroom.

What I find when I get there makes my pussy go damper. Declan is on his knees and David has taken the loosened belt and fastened it around his neck.

"Oh my," I murmur.

"To your liking?" David asks, sitting in the small armchair in the corner of the room.

"Very much so," I rasp, my voice thick with desire.

Layton and Ramsey stay out of my way as I approach the assassin in his submissive position in the middle of my bedroom.

"What to do with you?" I whisper, running my hand through his dark hair. I grip his chin and tilt his head back. His blue eyes are full of a longing that excites me, but at the same time, in some weird perverse way, turns me off.

"No," I say. "You want this too much. It was supposed to be something you were paying penance for."

His lips part in astonishment.

David snickers in his corner while Ramsey and Layton are silent on the other side of the room.

"Ooh, snap," David drawls. "On your feet, Irish."

Declan growls at him, but rises anyway, unfastening the belt around his neck. "Okay, Princess. What the fuck do you want from me?"

I hand the knife back to him. "Killer's choice," I murmur and turn around, hands behind my back, making it very clear that while he has all the power now physically, mentally, I'm steering this ship.

He throws the knife to Layton and then wraps the belt around my wrists.

"Do your worst," I whisper.

He spins me around and shoves his foot in between my feet, to part them slightly. Then I watch as he drops to his knees and lifts the covers on the bed to root around until he finds the box under there.

The big one, not the small one.

I smirk, suppressing the shiver that threatens to creep down my spine with fingers of ice. I'm completely at their mercy. Four men I can't say with any honesty that I know well, apart from David, of course, are in a room with me tied up and naked.

How will this go? As much as I want to think I've got the control here, it suddenly occurs to me that maybe I don't. Or it could be ripped away from me in a second.

My skin tingles, my nipples peak and the fear that slices through me is real. I shuffle closer to the only man in the room that I'm familiar with. David.

"Don't move," Declan instructs, pulling out an enormous sea green dildo from the box in the shape of a tentacle, complete with suckers on the underside.

I freeze, not knowing what to do. Suddenly, I'm not so sure about this.

"Cherry," Layton mutters. "It's your safe word."

My eyes shoot to his and I nearly drown in their clear depths. I nod, grateful that he knows exactly what I'm thinking.

Declan crawls back over to me and trails the dildo up the inside of my leg, giving me goosebumps. He reaches my pussy and circles my clit a couple of times before he shoves it inside me roughly, as high up as it will go.

I gasp as he lets it go and stands up.

"You want me to do something that I'm unfamiliar with, that you will enjoy and will prove to you how sorry I am for being a complete arsehole?" he asks.

I nod, my legs shaking from the pleasure the intrusive tentacle is giving me.

He holds his hand out for David.

My eyes go wide.

"I know your thoughts, Princess," he murmurs. "You wondered about this in the kitchen, didn't you?"

I nod dumbly.

"I have never been with a man before," he murmurs. "But never let it be said that I wouldn't do anything to keep my Princess happy."

"Fuuuck," I moan.

Layton, having stripped off completely naked and glorious, comes up behind me and picks up the knife from the bed where he threw it to get naked. He trails the cold steel down my spine.

"You up for this?" I pant to David.

He blinks. "Doesn't this fall into being non-exclusive?" he asks quietly.

"No," I pant. "If he was a woman, then yes. But here in this room...it's different."

"It's what she wants," Declan purrs in that accent that I know affects David as much as it does me. I've seen the interest in his eyes. "And we are all about pleasing our woman, are we not?"

"Yes," David croaks out and takes Declan's hand. He stands up nervously.

"You're going to have to guide him," I point out.

He lets out a soft laugh and it's all that was needed to relax him. He isn't the awkward one here, Declan is.

I watch as David takes a step closer to Declan. They are

roughly the same height, although David is much slimmer than Declan, barely a wisp next to Ramsey and Layton. Speaking of which, Ramsey joins me and Layton, also beautifully naked, his light skin marred with bruises across his ribs.

I gasp when he leans down to suck my hard, aching nipple into his mouth, biting down gently while he twists the other one.

Layton digs the blade into the skin of my back, hard enough to draw blood. "How does that feel, Cherries?" he asks darkly.

"Harder," I pant, my eyes riveted to David and Declan as their lips collide in a kiss filled with so much hunger, the dildo nearly slips out of me, I soak it that much.

Chapter Thirty-Nine

David

I stopped thinking ages ago. Or it seems like ages ago. The *only* thought in my head right now is that Declan is a fucking good kisser.

Man alive. He is making me all hot and bothered. The fact that he is a virgin in this area just makes it even hotter. I am under no illusions that we will have sex tonight, but I'm up for a blow job or two, especially if he is giving it to me. This man's tongue can work it.

"Fuck," I mutter against his lips, needing to have some verbal affirmation to his skill. "Ruby is one lucky lady."

She whimpers and I look over to see her trembling in between Ramsey and Layton. My blood turns to ice when I see Layton with the knife, carving something into her back.

"It's okay," she rasps. "Leave him."

I nod slowly, wondering what the fuck I'm supposed to do next. How can I stand here and let her be hurt in that way? I knew she liked it dark, but this is beyond what I'd imagined.

"David," she says steadily, drawing my eyes back to hers. "It's fine, I promise."

"Okay," I say softly. Who am I to interfere? I figure the best way to get past it is to dive straight into making it appear normal. "What are you...uhm..."

He gives me a twisted smile and turns her around so her back is facing me.

I gulp.

There, etched in her blood are our initials. He has marked her as ours. I won't lie and say that my dick didn't go on alert at that. Any other man now will have zero claim on her. She is *ours*. Forever.

"Fuck," I mutter again as he turns her back around.

Ramsey has taken control of the tentacle dildo and is thrusting it gently inside her while he rubs her clit with his thumb. Her eyes are glazed over, she is on the verge of a climax, but I can see why she hasn't exploded with arousal yet. Ramsey is edging her. He is building up her excitement, only to take it away moments later so she won't climax. I swallow and turn back to Declan.

I stare into those mesmerizing blue eyes and undo my pants. "I'll ease you in slowly," I murmur.

"Don't go slow on my account," he replies.

"Jesus," I mutter. "On your knees, Irish. Show me what you can really do with that tongue."

He drops and with a seductive glance over at Ruby, not me, he takes my already stiff cock in his hand. It drives it home that he is only doing this for her. Not that I'm in a position to complain. So am I. This wasn't something that I had planned on, nor expected. I knew that I had to have a conversation about my pansexuality at some point, but I figured it would be further down the line when that desire reared its head. I had no idea how that conversation would go, but finding a man in this way, wasn't how I pictured it would go. It's kind of perfect really.

Declan's mouth closes over the tip of my cock, and I groan as he twists his tongue around me.

"Oh, fucking hell!" Ruby cries out. "It's too much! Please, please!"

I pin her eyes with mine, leaving Declan to do his thing. If he has never given a bloke a blowie before, he is damn good at learning quickly. I groan softly as I see the raw lust in her eyes at seeing us this way.

Declan's soft tongue increases in pressure, and he starts to gently jerk me off as he sucks and licks me into a state of undeniable arousal.

"Quiet," Layton instructs her. "You are not to come under any circumstances. If you do, we will stop this immediately and you will be punished with an ice-cold shower. Tell me you understand."

"Yes," she pants. "Yes, I understand, Master."

At that last word, my cock bounces in Declan's mouth and I come in a flood of desire straight into his mouth.

"Uhn," I groan, closing my eyes briefly to enjoy the release before they snap open again at Ruby's cry of elation.

"Bad, bad girl," Layton tuts at her and picks her up, flinging her over his shoulder and stalking into the bathroom with her still climaxing around the tentacle, her body shuddering uncontrollably.

"I'm sorry," she pants as I hear the shower door open.

"No!" I shout out, realizing that he is going to make good on his threat. No...*promise*. Shit. Fuck. He really means it...

"Ahhh!" she screams. I lunge for the bathroom door to see her in the middle of the shower cubicle with Layton dousing her with ice cold water. She starts to shiver.

"Stop it," I demand.

"Safe word?" Layton asks her.

She shakes her head, her soaking wet hair plastered to her face, her teeth chattering. The dildo slips out of her and hits the floor with a loud thud.

"Declan?" I turn to him in panic. She is freezing.

"Not for us to interfere," he says. "She doesn't want it to stop. She wants to be punished. Don't worry about her. She knows when to call it quits."

I inhale sharply. I'm so new to this world, while not completely oblivious to it, I definitely had no idea these things happened. I thought it was all whips and blindfolds.

"Are you going to be a good girl again?" Layton asks her.

"Y-y-yes, Master," she chatters.

Layton turns off the tap and yanks a big, fluffy black towel off the heated rail. He bundles her up in it and gathers her to him, drying her off and then picking her up and carrying her back to the bedroom.

Once her body is dry, he whisks the towel away and picks up the knife again. "I don't want you to come again until I say so," he murmurs. "Next time, I will douse you with ice cold water and leave you outside for ten minutes in the freezing rain."

She nods, her eyes full of a heated fear that shocks me. She is so turned on by this at the same time as being afraid of what will happen. It makes me hard again seeing her this way. Always so strong, she is now in a submissive position and she's reveling in it.

"David," Layton says steadily. "Come here."

With my dick jutting out in front of me, and my pants around my ankles, I lumber forward.

"Go down on her," he murmurs. "When she is about to come, stop and suck off Declan while she watches."

I nod and drop to my knees. As much as I want to protect her, she doesn't need or want it right now.

The only thing left to do is give her what she wants.

Chapter Forty

Ramsey

I can't help it. I have my dick in my hand in a room with three other men, and the woman I love being treated as such that it has turned me on in ways that I never thought possible. Yeah, Layton was right to say that so far, my sex life has been vanilla. I thought losing my virginity at fifteen to my friend's mum made me hot shit in the sex department, but whoa. Layton has got a control over this situation that is fucking hot. Not that I'm thinking about him in that way, of course. But the whole situation is so hedonistic that the desire to come all over Ruby is pulling at me. I jerk off, my eyes on her pussy as David fingers her, licks her clit and then stops when she starts to whimper to turn to Declan and suck him off. Fuck, it's dirty. So dirty, it's scorching. I start to sweat, my good hand pumping my cock vigorously, ignoring the ache in my ribs.

There is a small, depraved part of me that wants Ruby to break the rules again. It's not me being mean, but instead a desire to see her punished. She *wants* it. There is no doubt in my mind that she broke the rules on purpose before. I saw it in her eyes before she climaxed so hard, I thought the dildo would snap in half inside her.

"Ruby," I pant.

"Come on me," she whispers. "If my Master will allow it."

"Go ahead. Cover her, see if she can hold out," Layton says, dropping to his knees and effectively cutting David off from seeing to her again. He concentrates on bringing Declan to a groaning climax with his mouth. I close the distance between us and as Layton leans back, I tug one last time and explode my cum all over her stomach and pussy with a loud grunt.

"Jesus," I rasp as the splats hit her skin and she shivers, biting her lip as she holds onto her own orgasm. Layton is quick to torment her, shoving the handle of the switch blade up her pussy and fucking her with it, while the blade digs into his palm, making him bleed.

"Master, please," she cries out, her shoulders shifting as the binds become uncomfortable for her.

"Release her," I murmur.

Layton glares at me.

"Tie her to the bed instead."

He chuckles. "Mm, I see your dark side has come out to play."

I help him get her onto the bed, face down so the marks on her back don't hurt. Then we spreadeagle and tie her wrists and ankles to the four posters of her big, fancy bed.

Layton resumes the dark fucking he is giving her, and she bucks, drawing her arse into the air as she holds onto her climax. I think this time she will try harder to abide. No one wants to stand outside in this downpour in January already soaking wet and naked.

"Declan," Layton murmurs. "Have you fucked her before?"

"No," he croaks out to my amazement. I'd figured they'd been at it like rabbits.

"Tease her and then I want you to fuck her."

"Do you want that, Princess?" Declan asks her, climbing on the bed and stroking her hair.

"Yes," she pants. "I want your cock inside me."

He holds his hand out and I bend down to look in the box, being the closest one to it. I pull out a soft looking whip and hand it to him. He rubs it against her clit before he slaps her pussy softly with it.

She sobs, but it's pleasure, not fear or pain that is driving it. I can feel myself grow hard all over again.

"Do you like that, Princess?" Declan murmurs to her.

"Yes, Daddy," she whispers.

I blink and take that in. Now I get it. Why he calls her Princess. I thought it was to do with her wealthy background, but it runs deeper and darker than that.

"I need her," I breathe out. "I need her."

Layton nods and so does Declan. They are giving her to me after they have worked her up. It will be the first time we have sex, and it is definitely way different than I imagine it would be.

"Take her," Layton says, "Take your woman and fuck her until she comes all over your dick and then make her lick it clean of her cum while Declan fucks her."

I nod. I don't know who made him the boss of this, but everyone is just accepting his instruction. Fine by me. I brace myself over her and ram my dick into her in one pleasurable thrust. Her soaking wet pussy encases me, taking in my big dick with ease because she is so slippery.

"Ruby," I pant. "Fuck you feel good."

Declan pushes his cock between her lips, and she sucks him off. He brings the whip down on her back and she makes a noise of agony as he lashes the cuts on her back, but she doesn't stop it. She lets him hurt her in a way that has to be torture for her. Why does she want this? It's something that I'm going to have to find out. She owes me an explanation and I need to know. I pump my hips, holding myself up over her as I ram my cock inside her, thrusting as high and deep as I can. Her cry is muffled round Declan's cock as she comes wildly, jerking against the binds that have her tied to the bed. Her pussy clenches around my dick, milking me hard and furiously. I groan and slam into her harder and harder until I burst inside her, detonating my cum into her pussy with a loud grunt. I pull out of her quickly, watching as Declan pulls out and then he moves away for me to shove my cock in her mouth. She licks me clean as Layton praises her and then he slaps her arse so hard, she screams.

Chapter Forty-One

Layton

The sound of her shriek sends a bolt of lust straight to my cock. If it wasn't stiff already, it is now. I slap her again, leaving a bright red mark on her arse cheek, which I then kiss softly and stroke gently to ease the harshness of my action. I narrow my eyes at the markings on her back. I want to talk to her about it, but now isn't the time. It was a bold move, maybe even an arrogant one and I hope she isn't pissed off about it. The scarring will be minimal. The wounds aren't deep, mere scratches, but I don't doubt they will remain etched onto her otherwise flawless skin for some time. It gives me a dark thrill that makes my cock bounce. I want her. Need her but I'm not giving in yet. She requires me to be this way for her a little while longer. She isn't ready to give up. I have faith she will inform me when she wants this to end.

It surprised me to learn that she and Declan have a DD/LG relationship. I knew she had someone else with whom she played but I didn't know it was that kind of role play. It makes me slightly envious, although when she called me Master and defined our own relationship in front of the other men, it pleased me a lot.

I cease stroking her arse cheek and slip off the bed to look in the big box of toys. She knows what she likes, that's for sure. I'm also fairly certain that the contents of this box are used in the place of a man, not usually *with* a man. She has suffered trauma in her life, something to do with being the Black Widow, and I hope one day she will feel secure enough with me—with us—to share her pain. It makes this all the more special, knowing she isn't one to open her legs for anybody. I pull out a huge black vibrator and turn it on to the highest setting.

"Untie her," I murmur. "And turn her over." I know her back will hurt, but I need her faced upwards for this.

David and Ramsey do my bidding, Declan having fallen into his Daddy Dom role and therefore not beholden to my instruction.

She hisses as her back settles on the silky sheet, but she opens her legs eager for more. Ramsey's cum is dripping out of her pussy and I use it to lubricate the tip of the vibrator before I press it to her clit, making her yelp with desire. It's a desperate, keening sound which turns me on even more. I rotate the vibrator against her clit before I shove it inside her and thrust roughly, fucking her and bringing her to the edge before I withdraw it and wait a few seconds. She growls at me, and I smile. She is close, so close to ending this.

I tease her again and then she's had enough.

"Cherry!" she cries and sits up before she launches herself at me, attaching her mouth to mine as she crawls onto my lap. She grinds down, reaching for my cock, which she grips tightly and shoves it inside her with a low moan.

"Yes," I murmur. "Fuck, yes."

Ruby rides me hard and fast, coming within seconds, clutching my cock fiercely with her pussy.

"Jesus!" she screams, throwing her head back and only giving me a few seconds to shoot my load into her before she's climbing off me and lunging at David like a woman possessed. I chuckle as she slams him back to the bed and climbs on top of him, pinning him down while he eagerly guides his cock into her. She fucks him hard and fast, gasping when Declan presses himself up behind her and pulls her from David before she has had a chance to come again. David groans with irritation, but starts to jerk himself off as Declan sits back with her on his lap and enters her so she can ride him reverse cowgirl style. I can't help but fall forward and press my mouth to her glistening clit, tasting all the cum mingled together. I nip her and tug gently which sends her over the edge with a cry of ecstasy that thrills me to the bone. I watch in fascination as she orgasms intensely around Declan's dick until he grunts and unloads into her, panting like he's run a marathon.

"Fuck!" he roars, thrusting higher as she stops moving, her breathing ragged. She smiles tiredly and twists on his lap, letting him slide out of her, to kiss him sweetly.

"Penance paid," she murmurs and then collapses in his arms. I take her from him carefully and cradle her as her eyes close.

"Bath first," I murmur. "I'll take care of you, sweetheart."

"Yes," she mumbles.

She is half asleep by the time Ramsey has run her a bath. I place her in it and carefully wash her, minding the cuts on her back. I enjoy this part almost as much as the sex. I run the washcloth carefully between her legs, knowing she will be sore and aching there after being battered by four huge cocks, an alien dildo and what I'm fairly sure was a vibrator in the shape of a horse's dong.

She moans softly confirming my thought and I pull away

not wanting to cause her any more pain. I drain the bath and grab a towel to wrap her in, picking her up and gathering her to me so she knows she's safe and secure.

Once dried, I leave her naked and tuck her into bed.

"Goodnight, sweetheart," I murmur, kissing her forehead.

She mumbles something I don't get but Declan does and is at her side in an instant.

"I'm here, Princess. I'm not leaving you ever again."

Daddy, she said. She asked for her daddy.

She smiles in her sleepy state and then she is out for the count.

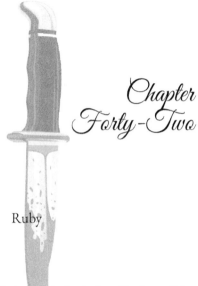

Chapter Forty-Two

Ruby

I wake up suddenly. Sitting up in bed, the silk sheet slides down over my breasts. I'm alone when only moments ago, my men were with me.

My men.

I smile, but it's quickly replaced by concern. I blink and then realize that it's light out. It was dark when I drifted off. I pick up my phone and look at the time.

9AM.

Wow. I haven't slept in that late since before my assault.

Climbing out of bed, I wince and hobble to the armchair to pick up my robe. I'm aching from head to toe, my back is burning, and my pussy feels like it was hit with a sledgehammer.

"Ow, ow, ow," I mutter, treading lightly down the hallway. Before I reach the sitting room, I hear Declan speaking quietly and stop to listen. I don't know why, but something about the tone of his voice makes me pause. It's soft. It's the tone he uses on me when he's pleased with me.

"I love you," he murmurs. "I'll be home soon. I promise."

My blood runs cold, but I'm not one to let things go. I like a good confrontation and he's about to find himself slap bang in the middle of a doozy.

Ignoring my aches and pains, I stride into the sitting room and snap, "Don't let me keep you from your lover, you dick!"

He turns, a look of surprise on his face, which turns to amusement.

I notice he is freshly showered and clothed in jeans and a t-shirt that is a far cry from the tux he came back here in a few hours ago.

He holds up his phone and wiggles it at me. "Eavesdropping, Princess?"

"You are in *my* home," I growl. "You don't get to have cutesy private conversations."

"What? Not even with me mam?"

I frown, and then feel like the biggest dick going. Which is saying something around here.

"Oh," I mumble, embarrassed at my outburst. "You were speaking to your mom."

"I was. But I love that you aren't passive aggressive about absolutely anything, darlin'. Aggression all the way is a major turn on."

"Fuck you," I drawl, but inwardly I'm smug. I'm also a bit marshmallow-y. He loves his mom and isn't too big of a man to tell her.

"So home is..."

"Dublin," he finishes my sentence. "Do you want to come?"

"Uh," I stammer, sideswiped by the offer. "Your mom probably doesn't want me intruding," I bleat like a fuckwit.

"She is dying to meet you," he responds casually. "And it's only fair. I know your father, after all."

"Yeah, and he punched you in the face," I say, pointing to his bruised cheek.

He chuckles. "I promise my mam isn't as belligerent as your da."

A tingle goes down my spine as he drops back into a broader Irish accent than he usually has.

"Can I think about it?" I mutter.

"Of course," he says and holds his hand out for me. "I've told her all about you though, so she'll be expecting to meet you soon."

I blush stupidly. "What did you tell her?"

"That I'm a man in love," he replies and leads me into the kitchen where the other three men are sitting with coffee or food.

I'm greeted enthusiastically, although none of them hug me. I know it's because they are aware how sore I am. It's sweet. And scary. I'm used to being alone. Not lonely though. I enjoy my own company. Now my kitchen, my *home* has been invaded by these men, but I find that I'm not that put out by it.

I accept the mug of steaming hot coffee that David hands me and pull away from Declan to open my laptop, which is already on the counter, courtesy of David, no doubt, to check my emails.

The first one that jumps out at me is a name that infuriates me.

"Giselle," I seethe and click it furiously to see what that cunt wants with me.

My narrowed eyes go wide and then I clamp my lips shut as I read her blackmailing email.

"What is it?" David asks.

"I'm going to fucking kill her," I roar and pick up my phone to hurl against the kitchen wall.

David's hand goes up and clamps around mine. "Sorry, no," he says. "New ones are a bitch to sort out if the old one is smashed to pieces."

"Grrr," I snarl when he wrestles it from me and hands me an orange from the fruit bowl on the counter instead. "Fucking cunt!" I yell and fling the orange as hard as I can at the French doors that lead to the back garden. It hits the double glazing with a thud and drops to the floor in a very anticlimactic manner. "And fuck you too," I grit out to the orange.

Declan bends to pick it up and tosses it in the air. Catching it, he asks, "Speak to us, Ruby. What's she done?"

"She is blackmailing me to lay off her," I snap.

"Blackmailing you with what?" David asks, perplexed as Ramsey comes closer with a concerned expression.

"She has recordings of me and my sessions at her club," I mutter.

"What?" Declan snaps, stalking over to my laptop. "How do you know?"

"Take a look," I mumble, and step closer so he can only see the first few seconds of the video I saw.

His face goes dark, and he growls loudly, turning to me when I slam the laptop closed.

"She's threatening to send that to my parents and plaster it all over social media," I say quietly, hating this, hating her and hating the way Declan is looking at me with sorrow.

"What do you want me to do?" he asks stiffly.

This must be having an effect on him as well, seeing the man he *murdered* abuse me in such a way that even a whipped dog had it better. How did I ever think that was okay? How fucked up am I? Tears spring into my eyes and David wraps his arms around me, and so does Ramsey.

Layton, who has so far been quiet—not unusually—stands up and says, "Tell us what you want us to do."

I pull away from the two men and brush my tears aside. How dare she think she can get away with this. She definitely doesn't know who she's dealing with.

"Nothing," I growl, finding my anger. I snatch up my phone from the counter where David placed it, ignoring his groan of protest, but I'm not going to chuck it this time. I scroll through my contacts until I land on the man I need to call.

He answers after a couple of rings and I snarl into the phone, "I've got a job for you. You know Giselle's in the city? Yeah? Burn it to the fucking ground and make sure it looks like she did it for the insurance. I want that bitch *buried*!"

I hang up in a temper and grip the phone like a lifeline, needing a release of tension before I implode with the rage coursing through me. She is about to find out that messing with me on this scale is a big, *big* mistake.

Chapter Forty-Three

Ruby

"**D**o we need to get in front of this?" David asks after a moment's silence at my bloodthirsty request.

"No," I state. "I need to shower and get ready for work. I will see you all later." I stalk off and then it occurs to me how rude that is. I turn on my heel and walk back into the kitchen, grabbing David and planting a kiss on his lips. I then turn to Ramsey and do the same, followed by Layton.

"I'll be here when you get out of the shower," Declan says before I can kiss him goodbye.

"Fine," I murmur and march back out of the kitchen and straight to my bedroom. I close the door and lean against it, my heart hammering in my chest. This is bad. Really bad. If Giselle makes good on her threat and sends those videos to my parents, I will be mortified. So will they. I'll never be able to look them in the eye ever again. But the worst is if it hits social media. My reputation will be destroyed. The hardcore boys club, which is very cliquey and something that I struggle to stay a part of on a daily basis, will see me as a weak, submissive *woman* that gets treated like shit by men and doesn't stand up for herself. They will see me at my most vulnerable, crying and shaking and *weak*. I will be ruined. I'll be run out of town and there will be nothing I can do about it. It's different for men, they'll be able to laugh it off and claim they love a strong woman and depraved sex, but *me*? I will never recover.

With shaking hands, I place my phone on the bed and strip off my robe, heading straight for the shower. My foul mood is lightened when I see the alien dildo still lying on the floor of the cubicle. I giggle and pick it up, throwing it into the sink and then turning the water on to lukewarm. As much as I want to blast my aching body with steaming hot water, the cuts on my back will sting like fuck and I'm not in the mood for self-inflicted pain this morning.

I'm quick to wash up and step out, grabbing a towel as my phone rings in the bedroom. I hurriedly dry off, walking into the bedroom and I scoop it up quickly. The caller ID makes my heart stop in my chest.

Mom

"Fuck," I mutter and wonder if I should answer it or not. I decide that there is no getting away from it if Giselle has already sent them the videos, so answer it breezily.

"Ruby," Mom's voice says urgently. "Have you heard from your father?"

I pause for a moment. "Uhm, which one," I murmur, forgetting about pleasantries as she did and feign ignorance.

"Rex," she says impatiently. "Have you heard from him?"

"Is everything okay?" I ask, my concern switching from myself to my mom.

"He said he was going on a business trip, but I haven't heard from him since. Do you know where he is?"

I debate my reply.

In the end, I have to protect myself. My dad can take care of himself. "No," I lie, knowing it's convincing because I've been lying to her for years.

"Dammit," she mutters. "Call me immediately if you hear from him."

"Will do," I chirp.

"Sorry, hunny," she says. "How are you?"

"Fine," I lie again. "But running late. I'll call you soon and we can chat."

"Okay, love," she says, and we hang up.

I grimace at the phone and fling it back on the bed.

"Fucking Giselle," I mutter and sigh, pushing it aside in order to get dressed.

Twenty minutes later, I'm dressed in a black dress that is tight fitting across my breasts because I discovered I can't wear a bra without it being too uncomfortable. The skirt flares a little bit but not enough that it swirls around me when I turn. As a result, I decide to forego panties knowing it will drive my men wild when they figure out I'm going commando. Picking up my phone and shoving it in my handbag, I make my way back to the kitchen. Declan is still in there, eating the squashed orange to my amusement.

I snort at him, and he grins. "Waste not, want not."

"Hmm," I murmur. "So speaking of homes..."

"Were we?"

"Now we are. Do you have one to go back to around here?" I ask casually.

"Not anymore. I live here now," he informs me.

My eyebrows shoot up. "You do?" I ask.

"Yep. I promised I would never leave you and I won't. So it's tough shit if you don't like it. And before you get your knickers in a twist...I'm not moving into your bedroom. I've unpacked my bag in the servant's quarters." He juts his thumb over his shoulder to signify the small but comfortable room off the utility room.

"That's for a live-in nanny," I splutter.

"Consider me your babysitter, then, Princess. I'm not going anywhere."

I sigh. What's the point in arguing with him? Besides, the fact that he took the live-in room means a lot. He could've just taken one of the two guest rooms or my room even.

"What about when you go to Ireland?" I ask.

"You're coming with me," he says confidently.

"I haven't decided yet," I reply quietly.

"Well, then. Mam will have to come here, and she'll be taking one of your guest rooms and making it her own... and don't get me started on this kitchen..."

I narrow my eyes at him. His baby blues are twinkling, and he knows he's winning this hands down.

"Fine," I grouse. "You win. Now can we go to work? I've got an appointment in an hour."

"Sure," he says and picks up his keys from the counter.

As we head outside, my phone rings and I answer straight away.

"Banker," I say. "What's up?"

"Our friend has paid his subscription," he replies.

"Very good. Please add him back to the newsletter."

"Will do."

"Also, don't forget to make a stop at Homebase. I need some fish food."

"On my way," he says and hangs up.

Declan opens my door for me, and I climb into the car.

"Fish food?" he asks.

"You'll see," I murmur, not trusting that his car isn't being bugged. Code is imperative when discussing things over unsecure lines.

He accepts that and we set off in silence. It's a good fifteen minutes later when he asks, "Are you okay? With the Giselle thing? I'm happy to take care of it. In fact, I *want* to."

"Don't," I say instantly. "I don't want any of you near this. Just let my guy handle it."

He nods slowly and then swears under his breath.

"What is it?" I ask.

"Checkpoint," he mutters. "The explosion yesterday must've spooked them."

"I'm not surprised," I murmur. "Let me do the talking, yeah?"

He glares at me, but I wave my hand dismissively. "No offense, *Irish*, but do you really want to open your mouth at a time like this?"

He growls. "That's not fair..."

"I know. But that's what they're all thinking about right now and IRA or not, you'll be igniting a fire that's already raging."

He hunches his shoulders, knowing I'm right. I don't want to be, and maybe I'm not, but better safe than sorry.

We pull up and after another ten minutes of simmering silence, we reach the front of the queue, and he opens the window.

The Constable leans down and gives us both a thorough looking-at.

"What's your business in the city?" he barks out.

"I'm Ruby Bellingham. A business owner," I say quickly but calmly. "Black Widows Bar & Club, amongst others."

He nods in recognition. "And you?" he growls at Declan.

"He's my driver," I say.

"Name?"

"Paddy McGuiness," he says shortly.

I bite my lip to stop myself from laughing. There is no way this Constable is going to let that go, especially around here.

He's going to want to know if Declan is the real deal comedian whose name he's borrowed.

The Constable leans down even further and scrutinizes Declan's face.

"Hahah," he laughs suddenly. "You're not him!"

"No," Declan says and reaches over to pick up his wallet. He pulls out an obviously fake driver's license and shows it to the Copper. "It's the bane of my life," he adds with a sincere chuckle.

"I bet," he says and pats the roof of the car. "On your way."

Declan nods and raises the window. I giggle. "Paddy McGuiness?" It occurs to me in that moment, this is the name he gave to my sister. I know exactly why he chose this name as his alias and why he chose to give it out now. I have no doubt he has half a dozen but disarming a policeman who is looking for trouble by distracting him with a laugh, is pretty savvy.

He shrugs.

"I get it," I say.

"Knew you would," he replies and then we are back to silence, but this time it's less uncomfortable.

Ruby

As soon as we step foot into the bar, David greets us. He hovers uncertainly and then bends to give me a quick kiss.

I smile up at him.

"So is it allowed?" he asks.

"Of course," I say. "But maybe not all the time."

He nods, happy with that and says, "I've swept for insects."

"Did you come across any?"

"Nope."

"Okay," I say and push open the door to my office. I'm greeted by a massive bouquet of flowers on my desk. I turn to David. "Who are these from?"

"Your appointment. He's running late because of the checkpoint. He wanted to stay on your good side, it seems."

"Nice," I mutter and walk over to inhale the pretty scent. I see that they're from the florist down the road, which is how they got here so quickly. "Send him in when he gets here."

"Will do. Also, the Banker swung by and left you a parcel in your bottom drawer.

"Thanks."

"Ah, the fish food?" Declan asks.

"Yeah. My appointment is for a loan," I say and sit down. I open my laptop and instantly it dings for a message.

I frown at it and then roll my eyes.

Thanks for throwing me under the bus, Rubes.

I ignore Rex's comment for a moment as Declan is giving me a curious look.

"Ask your question," I say.

"I didn't know you were also a loan shark," he says, a smile playing on his lips. "You've kept that quiet."

"It's not that well known. You have to know someone to get an appointment. That way I know who I'm dealing with, and if they don't pay, both parties go down."

"Nice," he says, his eyes lighting up at that nugget of information. "So it's kill the messenger as well?"

"Yep. That way referrals are given out only to those that the current loaner knows can pay. If they don't, they all find themselves without kneecaps."

"Interesting. What is your repayment on time rate?"

I furrow my brow at the question, but I trust him, so I continue to answer his questions. "Ninety-eight percent."

"Wow," he says, noticeably impressed. "Do you mind if I pass this on to someone I know back in Ireland?"

I nod slowly.

"I won't give them your name, obviously," he says with a tut, knowing the source of my hesitation.

"Can I ask who it is?"

"No one you know," he says and that is, apparently, the end of that.

Scowling, I turn back to my dad's message.

Sorry, I type. *It was kill or be killed.*

Nice. Stabbed in the back by my own daughter.

I can picture his face and I laugh. He isn't really pissed at me. But my mom will have torn him a new one for going AWOL.

Is she really mad?

Let's just say she knows where to fire where it hurts.

I crumple my nose up and try not to think about that one too hard.

How come you didn't call her?

She wouldn't understand unless I tell her everything. That's not my place.

. . .

Are you back in New York then?

Yeah, took the last flight out.

I spoke to Scar. She filled me in. FYI, it hasn't made a difference. Stay out of it.

He is no good for you. You know that.

Don't.

The three little dots come up and then stop while he thinks about a response.

A moment later it pops up.

You are not a stupid woman, Ruby. Don't let whatever vulnerabilities you have be swayed by him. He isn't your savior.

That's not what this is about.

It's a lie. He knows it as well as I do. I need to end this conversation before it goes someplace that I can't come back from.

. . .

I've got a meeting. I'll chat later.

I sign off before he responds by slamming my laptop shut.

I'm not a liar in that respect as there is then a knock at the door and David ushers in my client, a small, wiry ginger-haired man with a big smile and apologies on his lips for being late.

After twenty minutes of talking with this man, I'm satisfied that he can pay me on time and he is aware that if he doesn't, I will personally see to it that he doesn't walk again for a while.

I reach down and open the bottom drawer. Inside there is a small safe that is activated by a tiny prick of blood. It seems extreme, but inside is laundered cash, so not exactly something I can keep in my handbag. I wince as I place my finger onto the activation pad and then the safe clicks open. I pull out twenty thousand Pounds in twenty Pound notes and stuff it into an envelope. I hand it to my client.

"Sixty days to pay it back," I say and hand it over.

"Agreed," he says and takes it. He stands up and shoves it into his jacket pocket. "Thanks."

I shrug. I don't want thanks. I want my money paid back on time.

Watching as he leaves, I flick my eyes back to Declan. "Any chance you could leave me alone for a bit? I'm not a creature who enjoys being hovered over."

He narrows his eyes at me, but stands up. "I'll be in David's office," he says after a few moments.

"No hanky panky," I snicker and love that his cheeks go pink. How does the bad ass assassin get so embarrassed by a little sex?

"You're evil," he mutters.

"It's why you love me," I say and then freeze.

His eyes heat up and he approaches, sitting on the pleasure corner of the desk. "One of many reasons," he says and takes my hand.

"Say it again," I murmur.

"Will you say it back?" he whispers.

"Only one way to find out."

My heart is hammering in my chest when he leans forward and brushes his fingertips lightly over my lips. "I love you, Ruby Bellingham."

I smile and nip his fingers gently. "I'll come to Ireland with you," I reply and see the crushing disappointment in his eyes that I didn't tell him I loved him back. But how can I say that yet? I barely know him.

"Good," he mutters and drops his eyes to my lap. "You're being a tease," he adds darkly.

"Punish me?" I breathe.

"Let me think of a way while you have your alone time. I will make you pay, Princess."

I swallow, his tone leaving me with no doubt that whatever comes my way, my Daddy is going to be severe before he absolves me of my sins.

I can't fucking wait.

Chapter Forty-Five

Layton

I haven't been back in my apartment five minutes before there is a knock at the door. Suspiciously, I open it and glare at the arsehole on the other side.

"Boomer," I state. "What do you want?"

"Information," he says, looking shifty.

I don't think that he means to, he just has resting shifty face.

"I don't know what you're looking for," I say, exasperated. "There's really not much to tell."

"I told you that I want to know everything. If she masturbates, we want to know. So has she?"

"How the fuck am I supposed to know that?" I snap. "Look, all she's done is go home and work."

"And what has she done while she's been at work?"

"Work stuff," I retort.

"You're being very belligerent for a man whose life I hold in my hands," he chides me in a voice reserved for naughty kids.

I grit my teeth and try to be more amenable. "She spent time in the Widows casino and then she visited the other two sites. That's all I know."

"Do you know where she keeps certain things in the Widows casino?" he asks quietly.

"Like what?"

"Anything that isn't legal," he practically growls at me.

I'm pissing him off on purpose because I'm actually tired right now for the first time in years and I want him to go away so I can sleep. Being with Ruby has brought me such a sense of peace, I feel it's possible to relax and not be on edge all the time.

"Nope," I say. "I think we're done here."

I make a move to close the door, but he slaps his hand against it quickly.

"Nowhere near close to being done. Do you want to end up in jail?" he asks.

"At this point, I don't care," I grate. "Do whatever the fuck you want. We are completely done."

I slam the door now in his face and take great pleasure in doing so. It occurred to me in the last few seconds that whatever happens next, Ruby can protect me. I know she will without hesitation and while I'd rather she didn't have to, I know when I'm cornered. If Scott goes to the police, I'll get done. There is no doubt about that, but she has connections. She can get me out. My only concern now is for Linda. I pull my phone out of my back pocket and dial quickly.

"H-hello?" she answers quietly.

"Lins, I need you to listen to me. I need you to pack a bag and wait for me. I'm taking you away somewhere safe for a while."

"Wh-why?" she stammers.

Her voice is so weak, it makes me so angry. She used to be so full of life until her attack. It has destroyed her.

"Just do as I say," I mutter, trying to keep a calm tone with her. "Please. Something has happened and I need to make sure you are safe."

"What's happened?" she whispers.

"It's nothing to do with you, I swear. It's my problem, but I need to know that you are out of danger. Can you just do as I ask, please and I'll see you in an hour?"

"O-okay," she says and hangs up.

I don't know if Scott or Boomer will go after her to get to me, but I can't risk it. My tiredness will have to wait so that I can ensure she is as far away from here as I can get her and be back by midnight so that I'm not leaving Ruby for too long.

I bring up her number and dial, waiting for her to answer. She does in that sultry, sexy voice that gets me going like never before.

"Hey, stud," she purrs. "Shouldn't you be sleeping?"

I chuckle. "Not likely today. I have some personal shit to do. I'm not sure I'll make it back for my shift. Can you get someone to cover?" I get straight to the point because I know she will respect that more than me beating around the bush.

"Everything okay?" she asks, her voice now sharp and clear.

"Yeah, I'll tell you everything when I get back, but right now, I need to go."

"Go," she says. "Don't worry about this place. I'll sort it. Be safe, Layton." The concern in her voice touches me. I never thought I would have anyone who would care about me again. That fact that it is *her* means so much. She is fast becoming an obsession and for a moment, a shitty horrible moment, I rethink my plan to leave her.

"Dammit," I mutter and shake my head. I can't risk my sister for my own selfish needs. I make sure the knife that I've been carrying with me since Boomer first showed up is secured safely, but with a low growl, I grip the handle and pull it out of

221

the holster around my calf. Something has been gnawing at me since I carved our initials into her back. I need to do this, so she knows that she isn't just mine, but I am hers. I lift the sleeve of my jacket and press the blade against the soft skin on the inside of my arm. I quickly slice her name into my flesh, hard and deep to make sure it scars when it heals. I want her name on me, always. I need her that close to me. I wipe the blood away, barely feeling the sting of the cuts. I've been numb for so long, but I have a feeling this woman is going to change all of that. She is making me feel. She is taking over my rational thoughts to become the only thing I can think about. I have to make sure my sister is safe before I fall completely down the well of hunger I have for Ruby Bellingham.

I pick up my keys from where I threw them down only a few minutes ago and open the door. Boomer has dissipated thankfully, probably slunk back to his boss to inform him of my disobedience. Fuck them both. I have to do what I need to now and being threatened by those two scumbags isn't going to slow me down.

Chapter Forty-Six

Ramsey

S talling outside my apartment building, I tell myself it's because I'm making sure that no one suspicious enters. Although I do realize that if anyone was lying in wait for me, they would already be inside. It's not that I'm afraid of being abducted again. I'm more afraid of what Ruby will do if I am.

Huffing out a breath, in the cold late morning air, I take a step towards the road and cross it quickly, entering my building and heading for the stairs.

I take them slowly now, keeping my breathing steady. I feel around to my back where I stashed the handgun I stole from Ruby early this morning. I have never fired a gun before and never thought I would. They have been banned in this country since 1997, which is most of my life. I was only six when they were recalled and so never even thought about it really. Being involved with Ruby, and her underworld dealings changes the game though in a big way.

Layton would know how to use this. He was army trained.

SAS, even. But I'm not fucking asking him to show me. I'll learn by doing if I ever have to. But there is no way I'm giving this back to Ruby. She can try to protect me all she likes by keeping me sidelined, but the other day just proved that I can't be protected. Not that I want to be. I'm supposed to protect her.

I jump a mile when my phone rings and the echo around the stairwell spooks me. "Fuck's sake," I mutter and pull my phone out of my pocket.

Ruby.

"Hey," I say, trying to sound casual and not like my heart is about to burst through my chest.

"Why haven't you gone inside yet?" she asks to my surprise.

"You spying on me?" I ask with a raised eyebrow.

"Not exactly. I have little birds all over the city. One happened to mention that you have only just gone into your building. Your apartment is clear. You can go inside."

I scowl at the stairs, feeling like an absolute idiot. "It's not..."

"I know," she says, understanding in her voice. "But I'll want that gun back, you know. It's an illegally obtained weapon and you will get into such shit if you are found with it in your possession."

"Like you won't?" I retort.

"Of course. But I'm not stupid enough to carry it with me unless I have to."

"Neither will I," I lie.

"Ramsey," she sighs. "I want it back. If you insist on carrying a weapon, go buy a hunting knife or something."

I know she doesn't mean to sound like I'm some arsehole in need of supervision, but it sure feels that way right now.

"No," I say defiantly. "I'm not being the dick who sits around waiting to get abducted while you are running around out there with these dangerous fuckers everywhere you turn."

"I can handle myself," she says. "Besides, I'm going to show those dangerous fuckers that they're messing with the wrong woman."

"What does that mean?" I ask slowly, worry flooding my bones. She is going to do something stupid; I just know it.

"Doesn't matter," she clips out. "Now go inside, put the gun in the drawer of the table next to your door and go to sleep."

I growl my response, but she has already hung up. I grip my phone and shake it in anger. Not at Ruby exactly, but for her being so cavalier about her own safety, and I'm willing to bet that she hasn't told any of the other men about it either.

I quickly dial Layton, taking on faith that I can enter my apartment without anyone jumping out at me and slam the door shut behind me. I pull the gun out and test the weight in my hand while I wait for him to answer. When he does, it's clear he is driving and has put me on speaker.

"What's up?" he asks.

"Ruby," I grit out. "Can you do something about her?"

He lets out a loud laugh. "Like what exactly?"

"I dunno. Exert some of that control you have over her."

"Ah, dear boy," he says. "There is a time and a place for that, and her everyday life isn't it. What's she done?"

"It's what she's going to do. Or what I think she's going to do. She is going to get into trouble. Someone needs to stop her. She won't listen to me."

A pause.

"I can't. I'm on my way North. I can't turn around. I've got something to take care of. Call Declan."

"Fine," I mutter. I didn't want to ring Declan, but she has left me no choice it seems.

Not having his number when I hang up on Layton, not

bothering to ask what his cloak and dagger mission is about, I ring David instead.

"I need to speak to Declan," I say when he picks up.

"Well, hello to you too," David drawls. "How come? Why can't I help?"

"Do you want to restrain Ruby in her office so she doesn't do something that is going to get her killed?"

"Err," David mutters.

"Didn't think so," I grit out.

"I'll hand you over," he says, and I wait until the Irishman comes on the phone.

I relay my conversation with Ruby, and he says, "Hang on."

I tap my foot as I hear him walking to her office and opening the door.

"Feck's sake!" he roars, and my blood runs cold.

"What?" I ask in dread.

"She's gone," he spits out and hangs up.

"Fuck," I growl and shove my phone back into my pocket and the gun in the back of my pants. Any sleep I was going to get will have to wait. The troops are needed to save the beautiful, fierce headstrong woman we all adore from herself. I fire off a text to Layton. His business is going to have to wait.

Ruby needs us.

Chapter Forty-Seven

Declan

"**D**ammit, woman!" I growl and turn around to punch a hole in the wall behind me. It hurts like fuck and David is looking at me like I've lost the plot, but it's worse. I've lost my woman. I swore to protect her and now, I've let her walk into the lion's den.

I suck my bruised knuckles and glare at David's phone. "Unlock it and get Ramsey back," I snarl at him.

He takes it from me gingerly and does as I ask. Wordlessly, he hands it back to me.

"What did she say exactly?" I ask, exhibiting more calm than I feel. I'm not one to give in to rage. Well, not anymore. Rex saved me from that. He gave me a way to funnel all the anger and pain of being abused by my father for years, of watching him abuse my mother and siblings. I adopted a quiet rage and it made me a better sniper. *Makes*.

"Her words exactly were, 'I'm going to show those

dangerous fuckers that they're messing with the wrong woman'," Ramsey says.

"Fuck," I mutter. "Are you on your way back here?"

"Yeah, I'm here," he says, bursting into the office.

I blink and hang up. "Live close?" I ask, not really requiring an answer because it's obvious.

"Down the block," he confirms anyway.

I make a note that he hasn't broken a sweat, nor is he out of breath, even though he must've broken a world record in getting here in under three minutes.

"Jake?" I ask the room.

David and Ramsey both nod their heads in agreement. "Probably," David adds.

"Take me downstairs and open up that safe," I order David, pushing past him to exit the office.

"I can't," he says, jogging behind me to keep up with my rapid pace.

"You can and you will," I grit out. "Don't give me all that crap about loyalty. She needs you to look out for her now, seeing as she won't do it herself."

"It's not that," he replies. "I literally cannot open the safe downstairs. Only Ruby can."

"Fuck," I mutter again. "Why does she make everything so hard? Why does she feel the need to do everything herself?"

"Because she has never had anyone that she trusts enough to help her," he says quietly.

"Well, that has ended. She can trust us with her life."

"You know it," he replies.

"I've got this," Ramsey says, pulling a Glock out of the back of his pants.

I frown at it. "Where did you obtain that?" I ask, mildly impressed. He isn't exactly a timid man. I've seen him bounce the fuck out of plenty of arseholes who thought they could get away with shit in Ruby's club. But illegal possession of a handgun doesn't seem to be his style. I've been watching him, all of them for ages, so I feel I know him well enough to assume this. Well, except Layton. He is new and a relative unknown. That reminds me...

"I took it from Ruby's," Ramsey interrupts my thoughts. "We are playing with a whole new set of rules here. I needed to know that I couldn't be used as a bargaining chip for her again, but also to protect her if need be."

"Bold," I mutter. "You know she knows you took it, right? Nothing gets past her."

"Yeah, she's already read me the riot act," he grits out.

I take it from him. "Where is Layton?"

"On some personal business," he replies. "I texted and rang him, but he must've switched his phone off."

"What business"

"Dunno. He was driving somewhere."

"Hmm..."

"Wait," David says suddenly. "Don't you have your own... you know..."

I raise an eyebrow at him in question. "My own gun?" I ask.

He nods.

"Sure, but I can hardly walk up to Jake and shoot him in the face with a Barrett M82 sniper rifle, can I?"

"Well, no..." he says. "But you can take him out from the opposite building or whatever? Sorry, not up on distance shooting, or any shooting, for that matter," he adds.

"Do we even know where he is?" I ask.

"He is a financier in the banking district," David informs me. "6th floor of the Royal Exchange Building."

"Oh, really?" I murmur. I should've made it my business to know this, but he was never a threat before.

"What are you thinking?" Ramsey asks quietly.

"There is an apartment block on the opposite side of the

road. If I can get in and positioned in the correct place, I could take him out. But an operation like this takes weeks of planning. I don't know *anything*. I'm going in completely blind and that is dangerous."

"Then we don't do it that way," Ramsey says. "We walk in the front door. He knows David works for Ruby. He can get you in."

"How?" David croaks out, paling slightly.

"By being your usual charming self and putting that quick wit and sharp tongue to good use," I say, placing my hand on his shoulder. "All I need you to do is get me next to Ruby. I'll do the rest."

"Oh-okay," he stammers, gulping visibly. "What if they aren't there?"

I hold out his phone to him. "Call and ask," I say.

He takes it from me with a shaking hand. I know this isn't ideal. I would rather be as far away from that fat bastard as I can be to take him out, but I'm putting too much at risk.

"They aren't there," David says a moment later, hanging up. "Jake is at Perfect Ten's, the strip club on the other side of town."

I growl. "Dammit, Ruby," I mutter. This is just getting more and more difficult. That place attracts both men and women like flies to honey. It will be busy, even at this time of day.

"Actually, that could work," David says suddenly. "We could poison his drink or something and be out of there in no time."

I roll my eyes at him. Poison isn't exactly my style, nor my MO.

"No, this is going to have to get up close and personal," I say. "Ramsey, you drive." I throw him my keys and stalk out of the back door of the club, with David and Ramsey close behind me, as grim faced as I feel.

Chapter Forty-Eight

David

Sitting grimly in the tiny back of this fancy sports car, having been put here because I'm the smallest of our little band of merry men, I hunch my shoulders.

"You can't shoot him," I point out in the tense silence. "Not in there."

"I don't plan on shooting him," Declan says brusquely, which shuts me up.

I'm not asking what the assassin; the *killer* has in mind for our fat friend. I never thought I would get this involved in Ruby's underworld affairs. Part of me wishes I hadn't, but I'm here and I'm not going anywhere. I will jump in front of a bullet for that woman, I always would've, but it doesn't mean that I *want* to. I'd much rather have her safe and sound than be going on this mission to rescue her. Well, scrap that. I have no doubt she knows exactly what she's doing. She always does. I can see why Declan is so fraught, even though he is trying to hide it. He is paid to protect her, and from what I hear, he has done that. But it doesn't mean that she needs him.

"There's a roadblock up ahead," I mutter instead, "and then you're going round the one-way system the wrong way. We might need to circumvent the city and come in on the other side. It'll be quicker."

"On it," Ramsey says and makes a turn that takes us out of the city center.

"Won't we come across a checkpoint on the other side of town?" Declan asks.

"Not if you cut through where I tell you to," I say. I know this city like the back of my hand. I know all the nooks and crannies and alleyways and side streets.

"Tell me when," Ramsey says.

I nod, even though he can't see me. "So what do we think Layton is up to?" I ask, just for something to say. We've already established, we have no idea.

"Who knows," Declan growls. "But he should be here."

"He would be if he could," Ramsey says, defending his mate.

As if on cue, Ramsey's phone rings and he digs in his pocket to pull it out, and then he responsibly hands it to me to answer.

"It's Layton," I inform them. "His ears must've been burning."

"Or he's finally got my text," Ramsey says. "Answer it, for fuck's sake."

"Layton, this is David," I say into the phone. "I'm putting you on speaker with Ramsey and Declan here as well."

"Fine," he growls and waits. I think his natural voice tone is a growl. He's like a big bear. A big, *attractive* bear.

"Where are you?" Ramsey asks a second later.

"On my way to Scotland," he replies. "What the fuck has Ruby gotten herself into?"

"Who knows?" I reply glibly, even though this situation is anything but fluffy. "You coming back, or what?"

"Can't right now. I have something I need to take care of. I'll be back as soon as I can. Can you handle this without me?"

"I think we're covered," Declan replies with a tinge of sarcasm in his sexy accent.

"Don't let her get hurt," Layton says quietly.

"Layton? Who're you talking to?"

A woman's voice comes clearly over the line. The three of us go silent. Declan and I exchange a glance.

"That is not what you think," Layton growls. I wonder briefly if I accidentally put us on a video call. "She's my sister," he adds in a low tone.

"Oh," I mutter, feeling like a douche canoe for doubting him. Declan has no such issues though, and snaps, "Whatever you are doing with her, finish it and get your arse back here." He then takes the phone from me and hangs it up furiously.

"Don't you miss flip phones," I say with a dramatic sigh. "Nothing like a fierce snap to appease the phone rage."

Ramsey appreciates my comment with a loud snicker, but Declan ignores me and stares out of the window. I guess he is getting into kill mode, or whatever it is contract killers do. Although this isn't business. It's personal. Has he ever killed for revenge before? There are just so many layers to this mysterious man. I look forward to unpeeling them.

"Turn here," I murmur.

The atmosphere has become even more tense than before and it's making me uncomfortable. I loathe awkwardness of any kind, especially silences.

My heart hammers in my chest when a phone rings again, only this time, it's Declan's. He glances at it, scowls and then turns it onto silent

"Problem?" I ask.

"No," he replies shortly.

I roll my eyes. I love a mystery to solve, but he is hard fucking work sometimes. I think back to the kiss we shared and my mouth waters slightly. I wonder if that is a one-time thing only or will it happen again? Do we need to talk about it or leave it alone? I have all of these questions that have no answers, and I'm reluctant to bring them up in case I'm left disappointed. It's better to hope, than be crushed under the rejection.

I sigh and instruct Ramsey to turn again. We have hit the warren of roads on the outskirts and now it's time to work our way around and find Ruby before Jake hurts her. She was so stupid going into this alone. I know she doesn't care about getting her hands dirty and she can throw a punch better than most guys, but there is no way Jake will be without his goons. She is only one woman in a pit of vipers. There is no way she will get out of this unscathed.

Chapter
Forty-Nine

Ruby

With a look of disgust at the prostitute bouncing up and down on Jake's dick, reverse cowgirl style, I inhale a shallow breath. The stench of alcohol and cannabis in this place is overwhelming.

He knew I was here to see him and asked his ugly right-hand man to usher me into the Gold Room at the back of the strip club. He wanted me to see this.

Ugh.

He is such a pig. What did he think was going to happen? That I'd join in?

The bored looking, yet beautiful woman is definitely a pro. She has to be. No one in their right mind would screw this asshole unless it was for money.

She lifts up and rotates her hips, knowing her moves to get him to groan and work him up even more. She wants this over as much as I do.

He slaps her ass to my disgust, but she just rolls her eyes and slams back down on his cock, lifts up and slams back down. I can't help but look. It's like the scene of a hideous accident – you don't want to look, but that sick part of you can't look away.

I'm focused on seeing his tiny dick and then it disappears inside her pussy only to reappear again like the proverbial bad penny.

I lift my eyes when I feel her gaze on me and she smiles, slow and seductive. She licks her lips and then starts to pant heavily.

"Oh, yes, baby," she croons. "I'm coming...I'm coming... Ah, ah, ah..." She rolls her eyes at me again and I bite my lip to stop myself from laughing.

"Fuck, baby," Jake grunts and comes inside her.

I try not to vomit at the noise he makes.

She isn't bothered though. The second he is finished, she climbs off him and grabs her clothes from the banquet seat. She scoops up the wad of cash that has been left under her clothes and saunters out naked and full of Jake's cum.

I shudder. How can she do that? I mean, I'm not judging her choice of job; you do what you gotta do, but she is a stunning woman. Surely, she can do better than Jake the Snake?

"Rubes," Jake bellows at me. "You want a piece?"

"Ugh," I spit out. "You couldn't handle me."

"So I hear," he murmurs, which sets off my alarm bells. "If you aren't here for a shag then what is it you want?"

I blink and focus. "A deal," I say.

He stores his floppy dick away and zips up his pants. "What kind of deal?" He sits back and lights up a cigar. I resist the urge to choke on the smoke he blows in my direction.

"You stay the fuck away from my business and my people and I won't kill you," I state.

He lets out a loud guffaw.

"You've got sass, girlie, but you don't have the balls to get your hands that dirty."

I raise an eyebrow at that. Clearly, he has no idea the lengths I will go to hold onto my power in this city *and* to protect those close to me.

"Fact of the matter is," he continues casually. "...you're in a lot of trouble. Or you will be as soon as I send the police the recording I have of you blowing up that warehouse, so basically, you're screwed."

I clench my jaw tightly, but smile. "Hand it in, I won't see the inside of a cell."

He scoffs. "You're little DI won't be able to save you from an act of terrorism. Especially seeing as your business associate is the son of one of the most notorious top men of the IRA."

I narrow my eyes at him and take in the information on Declan. Interesting. It makes sense now why he was so insulted in the car earlier.

I put my hands in the pockets of my long trench coat. The idiot on the door of this back room only asked me to lift my dress to check I wasn't armed in the usual way. He didn't think to check for secret pockets within pockets in my coat. Of course, I lifted my dress a tad higher to distract him with my bare pussy and well, here we are, me armed and dangerous and Jake completely unaware of how much shit he's in. I wiggle my fingers into the small hole and grip the end of the Pangolin with my thumb and forefinger. Once I have a good grip on it, I stalk forward, holding my coat out with my hands still in my pockets in a show of who-gives-a-shit.

"You think my reach only goes as high as him?" I ask with a laugh. I pull my free hand out of my pocket and lean over him, grabbing his tie to pull him closer to me. Then I let go of his tie and walk my fingers up it, saying, "My reach goes *allllll* the way to the top of the city council and beyond." I bop him on his nose, making him blink before he goes puce. "Now listen up, asshole. You will back off my business and my people or I will end you."

He splutters while he gathers his bravado and then he gives me a disgusted look. "We'll see about that. You are nothing but a filthy, little whore. When everyone sees that video of you, you will lose any respect you had around here."

My blood runs cold, but I don't react outwardly. I'm not sideswiped by the revelation that Giselle sent him that recording of me, but it's not great news. I know what I have to do.

I whip the knife out of my pocket and press it against his throat, deep enough to make him bleed.

His beady eyes go wide, and he holds his hands up with a smirk. "Let's see if you've got the balls, whore."

Staring deep into his eyes, I slowly and deliberately draw the knife through the flesh of his neck, blinking as blood spurts into my face.

"What do you think about the size of my balls now?" I whisper in his ear as I slice his neck wide open.

His hands go up to the gaping wound, gurgling and choking on his own blood. I stick my tongue out and salaciously lick his face with a wicked smile.

I stand back and admire my handiwork, watching the life drain out of those insipid eyes, his pudgy face going gray as he dies in front of me.

When I'm sure he's gone, I grab a napkin from the small buffet table at the side of the room and wipe the blade clean. I shove it in my secret pocket along with the knife and ignore the phone buzzing away in my other pocket. I know it will be Declan. Ramsey probably went straight to him to tell him what I said, but it's too late. Jake didn't do as I asked, and now he is dead and out of my way. That just leaves Scott to make an example out of. I grab another napkin and clean the blood off my face as best I can, using the Champagne as an aid. I take a big swig of it and swirl it around my mouth before I swallow and slip out of the door past the lackey. I hastily yet casually make my way out of the back exit where my cab is waiting for me.

"Where to?" an unfamiliar voice asks me, locking the doors and turning to look back over his shoulder at me.

I narrow my eyes. "Where's Nathan?" I ask steadily.

"He won't be able to drive you today," the weird looking man says and then sprays something in my face which makes my vision go blurry.

I try to speak, but my tongue feels too big for my mouth. I struggle to get out of the car, but it's locked, and I can't open the door.

I slump and hit my head on the window and it's the last thing I remember.

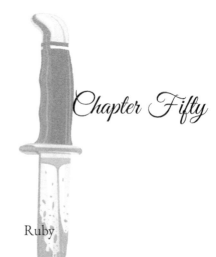

Chapter Fifty

Ruby

I 'm cold and my head aches like a cheap vodka hangover. I shiver, realizing that I'm not fully clothed. My eyes flutter open, the dank, darkish room, shedding little light onto my current whereabouts or predicament. My hands are tied behind my back, and looking down at myself, I can see in the dim light that I'm dressed in a very scant, black babydoll lingerie.

"Ah, you're awake," the creepy man says.

I look to where the voice is coming from but see no one until he flicks a lighter on and lights a couple of candles.

"Who the fuck are you?" I growl, shifting my position to keep him in my line of sight.

"No one you know, but your father knows me well."

"Which one?" I snarl, but it doesn't take a genius to figure out he means Rex, knowing what I now know about my bio dad.

"Don't play coy," the man chides me. "You know which one."

"What's your name?" I ask.

"No more questions," he snaps at me, but makes an effort to control his temper. That makes me think he doesn't want to hurt me. At least not in a rage. No, this guy strikes me as the precision type. It's going to hurt and be very damaging. "But I want you to know so you can scream my name when you beg me to stop hurting you. You can call me Boomer. Everyone does."

"Boomer," I repeat. "Scott's man?"

I've heard of him, but never had the pleasure. Thank fuck. This guy is creepy as all hell, and I really don't fancy my chances.

"My employer would like to extend his thanks for getting rid of Jake. Now he can fill that hole and then yours when you inevitably give up and pray for death."

"If you're trying to scare me, you don't," I spit out.

He chuckles, amused by that. "I can assure you, I do...or I will, soon enough. You, my girl, are about to witness my indelible talents."

"Great," I mutter. "Get on with it?"

"All in good time," he purrs. "First, I want you to stay very, very still. Don't move, barely breathe. If I see movement, I will start with your little finger, breaking it slowly and painfully. Do I make myself clear?"

I give him what he wants, and I don't move a single muscle.

"Very good," he says and smiles genially, which just makes him look even creepier.

He drags a stool in front of me, about six feet away and he sits on it. I try my best not to make an eww face when he unzips his pants and pulls his dick out. He is flaccid and small. I take shallow breaths when he starts to tug on himself while looking at me.

Ugh. This is sick, but at least he isn't touching me. It could be worse.

It's over pretty quick. He climaxes with a soft groan, spurting his cum out onto the floor and then zipping himself back up. He stays sitting down.

"You are a good girl, aren't you?"

I don't move or speak.

"You can be at ease now," he says, standing up. "Please rise and make your way over to the table." He points into the corner. It's too dark to see.

I struggle to my feet and walk slowly in the direction he pointed. My head swims. I felt okay when I was sitting down and still, now I want to barf while passing out. I gulp when I see an operating table with straps to restrain wrists and ankles. I need to get out of here, but panicking and trying to run won't get me anywhere.

"Climb on," he says encouragingly.

I do as he says. I'm not in any position not to right now. I slide my ass onto the table and wiggle backwards.

He comes around the back of me and cut the ties around my wrists. He rubs them gently and then guides me to lie back. I feel woozy and my head spins from being on my feet and staggering the few steps to the table. Whatever he hit me with in the car is still having an effect on me. I can't shake it off, which means I can't fight *him*. My arms and legs feel like lead. I close my eyes and don't struggle when he restrains my arms and then my ankles.

I want to run, I want to shout at him to stop, but I can't. I'm completely incapable.

"See how easy it is when you don't fight?" he asks, pushing my hair out of my face.

He removes his hand, but then I feel a sharp prick when he injects something into my arm.

I scream and buck on the table as whatever it was burns

through my veins like fire. Tears prick my eyes, and my breathing is a heavy pant.

After what seems like a lifetime of this agony, it disappears, soothed by another injection in my other arm.

"How does that feel?" he asks.

"Good," I rasp, giving him what he wants.

"Yes, very good," he says and then jabs me again with the burning hot fire, making me scream my lungs out with the torture this substance is inflicting on me.

I come to, not having realized I passed out. I don't know how much time has passed. It could be a minute, it could be several hours. I'm in a state of no pain, so am able to hear the light *slap-slap* as he jerks off. I turn my head towards the sound and get hit in the face with his cum.

"You're so pretty," he says. "You look so much like your mother."

"How do you know my mother?" I ask slowly, trying to steady my breathing and ignore the cum dripping down my face.

"My brother was in love with her for a long time. Your *father* killed him, so now I'm going to kill you so he can know the pain."

"What?" I choke out. "What are you talking about?"

"Revenge, dear girl," he says. "I'm sure you know all about it. You will die here by my hand, but I want to play with you first. You are such fun. I thought you would drop unconscious long before you did. So strong."

I blink. "What are you doing to me?"

"That's not important," he says. "What is important right now is that you call your men. I want you to tell them that you are fine and had to leave on family business." His vicious smirk sends the icy finger of dread down my spine. He holds up my phone and turns it on. He holds it to my thumb to unlock it and, wincing when I hear how many messages *ding*, he brings up David's number.

"They will know I'm lying," I point out. Declan, most especially, is no fool. I'm counting on him to find me, wherever the fuck I am. I wish I had some clue, but there is dead silence outside of this room.

It rings and then David answers, "Ruby? Where the fuck are you? Are you okay?"

"I'm okay," I say in the strongest voice I can. I can't give this demented asshole any cause for concern. "I had urgent family business. I can't go into it right now, but I'm okay."

"Okay," he drawls, not buying it for a second, but unsure how to contradict me.

"Listen, will you tell Ramsey to record the Man City match for me. You know how much I love them and don't want to miss a single game."

There is a slight pause which tells me that I'm on speaker and Ramsey is already listening.

"Sure," he says slowly. "I'll do that."

Now he knows I'm in trouble. They all know that I'm United all the way.

"I'll call again soon," I say and then Boomer hangs up. "Happy?" I ask, trying to find the fire that I know exists somewhere in me, somewhere.

"For now," he says and turns my phone off again. "I have someone coming to visit us. He is very particular, and you need to be silent and still or he will get very angry."

I nod, needing a minute to gather myself. I have to figure out a way to get myself out of this, because it doesn't look like the men have any idea where I am yet. *I* don't even know where I am yet.

A moment later, there is a soft knock on what appears to be a metal door. Boomer goes off to open it, and I watch his progress. Now I know where the door is. Although, I'm certain it will be locked up like Fort Knox. I hear scuffling and then a familiar face swims into view. I frown and it hits me in the heart like a speeding bullet. Surely, I'm hallucinating or something. But there again, I know how corrupt he is, so associating with the likes of Boomer here is probably all in a day's work for him.

"Oh, yes, she is perfect," D.I. Smith whispers, stroking my face.

I pull away, but he grips my chin tightly.

"Didn't you tell her not to move?" he asks Boomer.

"I did," he replies tightly.

"She is meant to be like a little doll. I don't want her moving," he sulks and if I weren't the object of this discussion, I would find it amusing.

"You aren't going to move, are you?" Boomer grits out.

I don't move or say anything.

I need to use this time to get my brain in gear, my survival is paramount now. I don't think D.I. Smith is interested in raping me. He has moved away. It's probably much the same as Boomer, masturbating while looking at me. It's creepy as fuck, but not exactly invasive in any way. I will get over it with a hot shower, a good scrub and a full night's sleep helped along by a bottle of the finest Scotch I can find.

"You have sampled her already?" D.I. Smith murmurs.

"Yes, she is a good girl."

He nods and drags the stool over to me. Boomer hovers over me and lifts the hem of the lingerie up over my pussy, leaving me exposed and vulnerable. Okay, this is going to be slightly worse than I'd hoped. He loosens the restraints around my ankles, but only enough to position me with my legs slightly open.

D.I. Smith lifts the holdall he has with him and drops it on the stool. He opens it and pulls out a sketch pad and pencils.

He wants to draw me.

Okay, that's not the worst thing in the world.

He removes the bag from the stool and sits, getting himself set up. I stare up at the ceiling and then feel the graze of a cold blade up my inner thigh. I freeze even more if that's possible. Boomer trails it all the way over my pussy to my stomach and then in a motion as quick as a cat, he stabs me in the gut with it, making me buck and cry out from the white-hot pain.

"Perfect," D.I. Smith murmurs.

Boomer leaves the knife buried in my stomach as I bleed out slowly and D.I. Smith sketches it. My brain goes fuzzy from the shock. I can't think.

My only thought is that I'm going to die here, and no one will ever know what happened to me.

Chapter Fifty-One

Declan

I punch the wall again, and then again. My fist is bloody and broken, but I don't care. I can't feel it over the pain of knowing that Ruby is in trouble, and I have no idea where she is or with whom.

"Well?" Ramsey snaps at David.

"Whoever she is with must've turned off the location services. I can't find her," David replies quietly. "Her last known location is Perfect Ten's."

"Where we know she killed Jake," I spit out. "This has to be connected."

"Not necessarily," David mutters. His face is pale and drawn, he is terrified.

So am I.

If I don't find her, my life won't be worth living anymore. She is the only thing tethering me to this life. *I* am responsible for this. I was the one meant to be watching her. How she slipped past the other eyes in the city on her is impressive and yet, now we have no idea where she is.

"I say we ring Rex," Ramsey says and then looks up as Layton finally bursts into Ruby's house where we have gathered to try and figure out where the hell she is.

"Where is she?" Layton demands, his face a mask of fury mixed in with fear.

"If we knew that, she'd be here," I snarl. "Where the hell have you been?"

"On family business," he replies tersely. "Something I'm starting to think was a distraction. It's not a solid lead, but I say we look at Boomer, Scott's guy."

"Why?" I ask.

"Because we parted ways earlier and I've had dealings with him before that made me think he was going to go after my sister. Instead, he went after Ruby."

I fly at him, grabbing him by the collar of his coat. "You mean this is about *you*?" I hiss at him.

"Again, not necessarily," David says, playing Devil's Advocate. "Maybe he just wanted Layton out of the way because he knows who he is, and this is all about Scott getting to Ruby."

I try to calm the fuck down, but I can feel that old, loud rage surfacing. I want to crush, *destroy* anyone and everyone in my path. I inhale deeply, trying to pull it back. The only way I know how is to let it all go. The darkness drops over me as I push whatever humanity is left in my soul aside and step back.

"Then we start there," I say, my tone dead to my own ears. "And when I find this fucker, I'm going to send him back to his mother in a shoebox."

The End

The 2nd Deadly Hearts book, Destroy, is available to pre-order: Destroy

The 1st book in Scarlet's RH Series: Crash is available to pre order: Crash

Don't forget you can read the Enchained Hearts Trilogy (the parents' book!) in Kindle Unlimited : https://geni.us/EnchainedTrilogy

Join my Facebook Reader Group for more info on my latest books and backlist: Forever Eve's Reader Group

Join my newsletter for exclusive news, giveaways and competitions: http://eepurl.com/gZNCdL

About the Author

Eve is a British novelist with a specialty for paranormal romance, with strong female leads, causing her to develop a Reverse Harem Fantasy series, several years ago: The Forever Series.

She lives in the UK, with her husband and five kids, so finding the time to write is short, but definitely sweet. She currently has several on-going series, with a number of spin-offs in the making. Eve hopes to release some new and exciting projects in the next couple of years, so stay tuned!

Start Eve's Reverse Harem Fantasy Series, with the first two books in the Forever Series as a double edition!

Also by Eve Newton

https://evenewton.com/books-by-eve

Printed in Great Britain
by Amazon